CHECKMATE
TO MURDER

CHECKMATE TO MURDER

E.C.R. Lorac

with an introduction by
MARTIN EDWARDS

This edition published 2020 by
The British Library
96 Euston Road
London
NW1 2DB

Checkmate to Murder was originally published
in 1944 by Collins, London

Introduction © 2020 Martin Edwards
Checkmate to Murder © 1944 The Estate of E. C. R. Lorac

Cataloguing in Publication Data
A catalogue record for this book is available from the British Library

ISBN 978 0 7123 5352 6
eISBN 978 0 7123 6707 3

Front cover image © The British Library Board

Typeset by Tetragon, London
Printed in England by CPI Group (UK) Ltd, Croydon, CRO 4YY

CONTENTS

Introduction   7

CHECKMATE TO MURDER   11

INTRODUCTION

Checkmate to Murder was published in 1944, when E. C. R. Lorac was at the peak of her powers. This domestic murder puzzle captures the febrile atmosphere of wartime, a period of British history when blackouts, fire-watching, and air raid precautions were an everyday fact of life.

The story opens on a foggy evening in London. A group of people are to be found in or around the large Hampstead studio of artist Bruce Manaton. At one end of the fifty-foot-long room, Manaton is painting the portrait of an actor, André Delaunier, who is resplendent in the scarlet robes of a cardinal. At the far end, two men are hunched over a game of chess. They are Robert Cavenish and Ian Mackellon, both of whom are highly respectable individuals who work for the government. Rosanne Manaton, sister of Bruce and also an artist, who is cooking supper in the adjoining kitchen, occasionally pops in to the studio. A cleaning lady, Mrs Tubbs, is also bustling about the place. Everything seems calm, but this peaceful scene is about to be interrupted by murder, and before the end of the story the lives of several of those present will be changed forever.

Suddenly a special constable bursts in on the gathering. He tells Manaton and the others that he has chanced upon a body in the next door building. The dead man is called Folliner; he was a miser and his money has gone missing. Verraby, the special constable, believes he has already caught the murderer—a young Canadian soldier who is a great-nephew of the victim and who made a run for it when he was about to be arrested. When Verraby hands the culprit over to the official police of Scotland Yard, it seems that he has presented them with an open-and-shut case.

Lorac's series investigator, Detective Chief Inspector Macdonald, nevertheless suspects that all may not be as it seems. Macdonald is shrewd and compassionate, but also relentless. As he and his team delve deeper, they uncover a tangle of potential motives. Even the behaviour of the special constable is open to serious question—are his dabbling in property speculation a clue to the crime? And what really did happen to the old man's money?

The war-time setting and atmosphere are integral to the mystery. As Bruce Manaton says, "Londoners have heard so many bangs during their recent history, that a pistol shot isn't so impressive a row as it used to be." Macdonald agrees: "I suppose all Londoners who survived the winter of 1940 with nerves unimpaired, did develop what the psychologists call a 'defence mechanism'—they learned to disregard disessential bangs."

Today, more than three-quarters of a century later, it is fascinating to read an account of a domestic crime committed at a time of national crisis. A minor character called Miss Stanton expresses the prevailing mood: "Bombs I can disregard—we're all in it together—but crime and corruption and disreputability—it's too much."

Caroline Rivett, who wrote both as E.C.R. Lorac and as Carol Carnac, was herself a Londoner. Born in Hendon in 1894, she attended the South Hampstead High School and the London School of Arts and Crafts. She published her first detective novel in 1931; this was *The Murder on the Burrows*, a well-crafted debut which launched Macdonald on a career that was to last for more than a quarter of a century.

Nine Lorac novels were published by Sampson Low, earning increasingly favourable reviews, before she moved to the more prestigious imprint of Collins Crime Club in 1936, with *Crime Counter Crime*, set during a General Election. She remained a Crime Club stalwart for the rest of her life. John Curran, historian of the Crime Club, argues that she was especially well served by the designers of the cover artwork for her books, and this is no doubt one of the factors that has made her work especially collectible. First editions in the attractive dust jackets of the period can now change hands—on the rare occasions when they come on to the market—for thousands of pounds.

She was equally at home with urban and rural settings. Her early books include *Murder in St John's Wood* and *Murder in Chelsea*, while two other books set in London, *Bats in the Belfry* and the war-time mystery *Murder by Matchlight*, have already been published in the British Library's Crime Classics series. Like Rosanne Manaton, she was artistic and had an interest in ski-ing; the winter sport plays a central part in her Carol Carnac novel *Crossed Skis*, also published by the British Library.

In November 1940, having been evacuated to Devon, she wrote to a friend about the horrors of living through a war. Referring to the death of one of her oldest friends, killed while fire-fighting, she said: "Most of my other friends have been bombed or burnt out of their homes. What a sickening insanity it all is."

By the time *Checkmate to Murder* was published, she had moved up north, to Aughton in Lancashire, to be near her sister Maud and brother-in-law John Howson. They are all now buried in the graveyard at Aughton church, along with a third sister, Gladys. In the years before her death in 1958, Carol Rivett became a popular figure in the village while continuing to work productively as a detective novelist. To this day, she is remembered in the local community as spirited and strong-willed, a woman with a strong social conscience. Macdonald, a quiet but utterly single-minded detective, embodies both her determination and her humanity.

MARTIN EDWARDS

www.martinedwardsbooks.com

CHECKMATE
TO MURDER

CHAPTER ONE

I

THE VAST STUDIO HAD TWO FOCUS-POINTS OF LIGHT; BETWEEN these pools of radiance was a stretch of shadows, colourless, formless, empty. At one end of the long, barn-like structure, where the light was most strongly concentrated, was a model's platform. A high-backed Spanish chair stood upon it, with a dark leather screen as background. On the chair sat a man arrayed in the superb scarlet of a Cardinal's robe, the broad-brimmed Cardinal's hat upon his head.

The lights were so arranged that they illumined the pale haughty face of the sitter, his challenging black eyes and beetling brows. Beneath his square powerful chin was a triangle of ecclesiastical purple—magenta described it more truly. His sleeves were lined and edged with cerise silk—a gorgeous clash of colour discord contrasting with the heraldic scarlet of the frock. One powerful white hand gripped the arm of his chair: the other hand rested on the jewelled cross on his breast.

Opposite to the sitter, at a distance of some ten feet, a painter's easel supported a six-foot canvas, and the painter stood before it, blocking in his drawing in charcoal. He wore an overall of vivid butcher's blue which made his pale face, with its sharply hewn profile, paler still. The face was heavily lined, the eyes set deep in their sockets, their shadows intensified by the strong light. Painter and sitter, both illuminated by the same set of lights, made one composition of startling primary colour, challenging and arresting.

At the farther end of the fifty foot studio, separated from the painter and his model by the shadows which claimed the greater part of the floor-space, was another group, lower-toned, yet still of pictorial value.

Close to the stove, lighted by an electric bulb hanging immediately over their heads, two men sat on either side of a chess-board. One—the younger of the two—was a tawny-haired fellow, whose hair shone under the light. He had taken off his tweed coat and sat in a Fair Isle pull-over of green and russet and ochre, his long legs clad in brown corduroy slacks. His opponent at the chess-board was an older man, white-haired, dressed in a conventional dark lounge suit. Both men sat with their elbows on the table, their chins on their hands, utterly concentrated on their game. The beam of light which was directed down on them was shaded so that its rays did not reach the rest of the studio: the smoke from their pipes coiled up in blue wreaths, and the two players, with the board between them, achieved a sort of pattern whose composition was so precise that it seemed the result of deliberation rather than chance.

For the greater part, silence reigned in the studio. The chess players had been intent on their game for a full hour, and an occasional low-spoken "check" came from one or the other, and then a long pause as each considered the next move. Robert Cavenish, the older of the two players, sat almost immobile, a frown of concentration furrowing his fine brow as he brooded over the pieces. Ian Mackellon, tawny-headed, long-limbed, spare, a typical Scot, moved his long legs occasionally as though he were cramped at the table, and sometimes he cast a glance at the vivid robes of the Cardinal on the model's platform. There was the glint of a smile in his deep-set blue eyes, light under their heavy brows, as though the game were going well for him, and his eyes moved back to the board with a half-smiling concentration.

At the farther end of the studio, Bruce Manaton stood at his canvas, drawing with a sort of savage determination, as much wrapped up in his task as were the chess players. Occasionally he uttered a curt admonition to his sitter, when the latter changed his pose a little as he tired.

"Chin up, chin up—to the right a little—" the low-toned, rather irritable voice punctuated the silence as did the chess players with their monotonous challenge, and the Cardinal would raise his head and recover his poise, still with the same expression of gloomy haughtiness. André Delaunier—he who was clad in the Cardinal's scarlet—was an actor by profession, well accustomed to posing, but he demanded a rest occasionally. Once, during the first hour of the chess players' game, he had stood up impatiently, heedless of Manaton's irritation, and had stalked majestically across the intervening gloom to stand behind the players and to con the board, while he stretched out his shapely white hands to the stove, to catch its warmth. The month was January, the temperature outside below freezing point, and the acrid London fog seeped in to the studio, a faint sulphurous reminder of the grimy blanket which enwrapped the whole Thames basin in noxious stillness.

As Delaunier stood considering the board, neither player acknowledged his presence by word or movement, and the actor stood with a derisive smile on his lips as he observed the trap Mackellon was contriving for the older player. Manaton's brusque voice recalled him.

"Either you're posing or else you're playing chess," he said. "You can't do both."

"Damn you, for the devil's own slave-driver," retorted Delaunier.
"If I can't move occasionally I shall just coagulate into a lump. All
right, all right—don't lose your wool," he concluded good-temperedly,
as Manaton threw down his charcoal with an irritable gesture.
Delaunier strode back silently across the studio, only the swish of
his heavy robes making his passage audible, and he sat down again
in the high-backed chair, resuming his former pose with the skill
of the actor who donned his part as easily as he donned a garment.

Neither of the chess players had moved or spoken during the
sitter's interlude. Cavenish showed by a deepening of the furrow
between his brows that he was ignoring the interruption by a
conscious effort, but Mackellon, his half smiling eyes on the chess-
board, seemed aware of nothing but the ivory and ebony pieces of
the game.

"Check," he said again.

II

During the course of the sitting Rosanne Manaton occasionally
looked in at the studio from the door which led into the kitchen.
The latter was a small room built as a lean-to against the studio wall.
In size, the "kitchen" was spacious in comparison with the kitch-
enettes to be found in most small modern flats, but Rosanne, who
was a fastidious creature, had looked at the domestic offices of the
studio with unconcealed disgust when she had first seen the place.
The "kitchen" was also the bathroom, and when Rosanne and Bruce
Manaton had inspected the property with a view to renting it, the
"k & b," as Rosanne called it, had nearly overcome her determination to get settled at any price into some quarters which she and

her brother could call their own. The scabrous peeling walls, the rusty bath and the beetle-infested floor had filled her with loathing.

"It's ghastly, Bruce," she had said.

"Oh—what matter? We can soon clean it up. It's the studio that matters, and that's damn good," he had replied.

It was Rosanne, of course, who had done the cleaning. The Manatons had had no money to spare for decorators. They oscillated between two initialled states—"B" and "A.B," "Broke" and "Absolutely Broke." Rosanne was an etcher and wood engraver, and her sensitive imaginative work had had some financial success in peace time: since the war her earnings, and those of her brother, had contracted to negligible amounts. The rather derelict studio in Hampstead had had cheapness to commend it, and Rosanne was always prepared to make the best of her surroundings. It was she who had first scrubbed down and later distempered the kitchen walls, re-enamelled the bath and sand-papered the rusty gas stove. She was still in process of redecorating the studio, intolerant of its dirt and dreariness. Bruce just shrugged his shoulders and left her to it. Grimy walls troubled him not at all. "I've seen worse in Paris," was his only comment.

Rosanne, standing looking at the studio and its occupants, was intensely aware of the decorative quality of both of the groups in it on that foggy winter evening. She did not often paint herself now: line work was her medium, but she felt an impulse to indulge in a modern composition in which both chess players, painter, and sitter should form a pattern, irrespective of distances and planes. With one hand on her hip, the other resting against the edge of the door, Rosanne Manaton herself achieved something in the way of a design, though she was all unconscious of it. Tall, lithe, dark haired, clad in an old ski-ing costume which she had put on for its cold-resisting

qualities, Rosanne was an unusual figure. The costume suited her
long slender body. Very few women past the age of thirty look well in
trousers, but the black ski-suit, with a vivid scarlet scarf at the neck,
became Rosanne's long-limbed slenderness, as her close-cropped
black hair became her shapely head. Beautiful she was not, but she
had a quality best described by the word grace. Every movement of
body or limbs, hands or feet, had the same characteristic of beautiful
balance and efficiency. She moved purposefully, with an economy
of effort in which no movement was redundant.

As she stood looking at the studio, brooding over its pictorial
possibilities, her brother turned irritably from his canvas and called
to her:

"For God's sake either come inside or go right out, and shut that
damned door. It's draughty enough in here anyway—and I don't
want a cross light."

Rosanne withdrew into the kitchen and closed the door behind
her. She was used to her brother's irritable and often mannerless
ways, and ignored his captiousness. Bruce was always at his most
disagreeable when he was working.

Rosanne returned to her cooking. She had undertaken to produce supper for five people at nine o'clock. The chess players and
Delaunier had each provided a ration of something "to put into the
pot," and Rosanne was contriving a savoury stew from the miscel-
laneous collection brought in by the others, added to the meat and
vegetables she had bought for herself. Actually she loathed cooking,
but with the rare common sense which characterised her, she had
taught herself to cook, and to cook well, in order to prevent Bruce
squandering their slender means on restaurant meals. Rosanne, side
by side with her natural artistry, had a sense of orderliness which
made her intolerant of what she called "money messes." She did

not resent poverty so much, but she could not bear the squalor of indebtedness and constant borrowing which seemed to come so naturally to her brother.

As she stood by the gas cooker, studying her simmering pot, someone knocked on the door which opened from the kitchen into the sooty garden in which the studio building stood. Rosanne pulled down a shade over the bare electric bulb before she opened the door. Black-out regulations were a nightmare to her, because her impatient brother was always forgetting them, and the probability of being fined always hung over their heads.

She opened the door carefully, saying,

"Is that you, Mrs. Tubbs?"

"That's me, dearie," replied a cheerful Cockney voice, and a short wizened little woman negotiated the entrance and squeezed herself into the kitchen.

"Lor'! You give me quite a turn seeing you in that outfit," said Mrs. Tubbs. "Jest like your brother you look, the dead spit of him. I got you a coupla' pairs of lovely 'errings orf the barrow as I passed. You can't beat 'errings for food value, and tasty at that."

"You know, you *are* a dear, Mrs. Tubbs! You're always doing me a good turn—"

"Bless you, dearie, that's all right. Don't you go bothering your head being grateful. I just popped in to say I'd come and lend you an 'and with the scrubbing to-morrow. What time can you get that brother of yours out of the way? 'E do *fuss* so. Can't bear menfolk worriting round me when I'm working, and that's flat."

"He's going out at ten to-morrow morning, Mrs. Tubbs."

"That'll suit me fine, dearie. I shall have time to pop in and look at my old bundle of misery and then I'll come on to you for an hour or two, just as *you* likes."

"I shall be jolly glad to have you. That studio floor is interminable, and most of it's still filthy. I'm afraid it's a rotten job for you, though, and I'm ashamed I can't afford to pay you any better."

"Now that's all right, dearie. I'm doing fine, with me old man in the P.B.I. same as he was before, and me daughter in munitions. 'Mum,' she says to me, 'why don't you stop at 'ome, like a lady, with me making good money and that?'—but bless you, dearie, it don't come natural just stopping at 'ome. I always done a spot of work, and I'm used to it. As for my bit of bother up there—" and she jerked her thumb expressively over her shoulder, "it ain't what 'e pays me, that wouldn't keep a flea, it's just I can't bear the thought of 'im living alone and no one going in to see if he's alive or dead."

Rosanne shuddered a little. "You mean old Mr. Folliner? I thought he was a horror. I went in to see him when my brother and I took the studio, and he made me feel just as I did when I saw the black beetles on this floor—all creepy-crawly. He's a miser, too, isn't he?—horrible old skinflint."

"He's all that, dearie, with knobs on. Getting worse, he is, too. Breaks 'is wicked old 'eart to part with a penny. Still, what I says is, we may all be old 'orrors in time, if we're spared. I known 'im ten years, and 'e wasn't that bad once. Anyway, I said to me 'usband, 'Alf,' I says, 'I'm going to see 'im out, and I'll lay 'im out wif me own 'ands if 'e dies on me, but see to 'im I must. Can't leave 'im all alone like that, day after day.'"

"Well, I call it jolly decent of you. There wouldn't be many people who'd bother about him. You've got more Christian charity than I have, Mrs. Tubbs."

"Now don't you mention them two words to me, dearie. Charity I can't abide, and as for a Christian, I'm a proper 'eathen. I ain't been to church since I went when me first was christened, and that one

died within the year, and I said 'What's the good of it, any old 'ow?'
Now I must just pop off. See you in the morning, and remember
you do them 'errings in oatmeal, same's I told you. Lawks! What a
night. Not fit for a dog to be out, and that's flat."

The cheerful old body squeezed herself out of the door, and
Rosanne stood and mused for a moment, marvelling over the kind-
ness of Mrs. Tubbs and her like. It seemed to Rosanne that there was
more genuine goodness to be found among the poor and illiterate
than among all the intellectuals who posed as her brother's friends.

Before dishing up the supper, Rosanne decided to go outside to
see if the studio black-out were really efficient. She had contrived
screens for the big north light and was always afraid that they would
fail in their purpose. Screening the kitchen light again, she slipped
out into the garden and the fog closed round her like a blanket.

III

"Smells good, Rosanne, and by God, I'm hungry. Who thought to
bring the beer? Delaunier? Good for you. Well—here's luck. We
need it."

The party of five were seated round a table near the stove, and
Rosanne, with Delaunier on her right and Cavenish on her left, was
ladling out the stew. She paused a moment, the ladle in mid-air, and
listened.

"There's someone outside. I was certain I heard something when
I went out ten minutes ago."

"Why go outside on an evening like this?" asked Delaunier.
"Hades itself couldn't be worse. I loathe fog more than anything
on earth."

"I went out to see that there weren't great chinks of light shining out from the north window," said Rosanne, and Cavenish put in,

"No one need be afraid of raiders on a night like this. Fog immobilises them completely."

"I'm not afraid of raiders. I'm afraid of being fined five pounds when I haven't got it to pay," retorted Rosanne. "We've had air-raid wardens in here complaining several times already."

"Oh, to hell with them," said Bruce impatiently, and Ian Mackellon put in:

"I say, there *is* a shemozzle of sorts going on outside. I'll go out and see what it is. Perhaps an air-raid warden's staggered into the dug-out."

"Let him drown, then. The damn fool thing's brim full of rain water," replied Manaton, and Mackellon jumped up just as someone thumped on the studio door. Bruce Manaton got to his feet swearing angrily, and Rosanne cried out,

"Switch the big light off before you open the door."

"What a life," said Cavenish, and his eyes met Rosanne's with kindly sympathy. Delaunier sat still in his place, superb in his Cardinal's scarlet, but with a glass of beer in one hand, looking oddly unnatural in contrast with the ecclesiastical trappings. An altercation was going on at the main door of the studio.

"There isn't a telephone, so it's no use trying to be high and mighty." Bruce Manaton's resonant voice was clearly audible. "We're poverty-stricken painters here, not plutocrats with telephones. If you want to 'phone go to the post office—first on the right and third on the left."

"… represent the law… demand your assistance…"

A stuttering breathless voice answered Manaton's impatient tirade and Mackellon put in:

"What's the poor devil done, anyway?"

Rosanne jumped up and ran to the door. A screen kept the light from the doorway, and in the dimness she had a confused impression of a tall grey-headed man in navy blue who seemed to be grasping a lad in khaki, the latter tallow-faced, and leaning against the door post, panting.

"Why not come inside and explain?" asked Rosanne. "If there's been an accident we will do our best to help."

"Accident? There has been a dastardly crime, a deplorable outrage." The big man in dark blue was getting his breath back. "I must summon assistance, and I have the right to call on all law-abiding citizens to assist me in my duty. I have arrested this miscreant—"

"Oh come off it, and don't try any more jargon on me," said Manaton flippantly, and Rosanne put in quickly,

"Well, whether you've arrested him or not, why not come in and shut the door, and he looks half dead himself anyway."

"I've twisted my damned ankle so that I can't stand," put in the lad in khaki. "If it weren't for that I could have got away."

"I call you to witness that statement," said the grey-headed man. "Come inside, quietly now. Resistance will do you no good. You are under arrest, and I warn you that anything you say may be taken down in writing and used as evidence."

He propelled the soldier inside and banged the door to behind him. Rosanne saw that he was in the uniform of a special constable, a big prosperous-looking man of sixty. The Tommy winced as he tried to put his foot to the ground and staggered, and Mackellon shoved a chair forward saying:

"Let him sit down anyway. He's all in."

Delaunier strode forward in his Cardinal's scarlet, and his appearance added the last touch of fantasy to the group: the Tommy looked bemusedly from the scarlet figure to Rosanne, tall and slim in her black ski costume.

"It's not real—I must be dreaming," he said, "or else I'm mad… the whole show's stark crazy."

"What the hell is it all about?" demanded Manaton, and the Special Constable replied:

"A dastardly murder has been committed in the house adjoining this studio. I have arrested this man—arrested him red-handed—and I must see that he is secured before I summon assistance. Is there a cellar or other apartment where he can be locked up? I shall hold all of you persons responsible for him, remember."

"Who has he murdered, anyway?" demanded Manaton, and the Tommy burst out:

"I haven't murdered anyone, I tell you. I don't know a damned thing about it. Someone else did the old man in—not me."

He was a Canadian, Rosanne noticed, very young, his fair face tanned, but pallid and drawn.

"Silence!" commanded the Special Constable. "There is to be no discussion at all. I asked *you*, sir, about a cellar or other apartment suitable for a lock-up. I have no time to waste on arguing."

"And I have no cellar, nor yet any apartment suitable for a lock-up," replied Manaton coolly, and Cavenish spoke for the first time.

"Look here, sir. It's no use talking about lock-ups in a studio which hasn't a single door which locks properly. Leave this chap here while you go and telephone or find another officer. There are four of us here, and he can't get away. He's obviously in no state to get away, and he can hardly stand, let alone run."

The big grey-headed man seemed to be mollified by the quiet voice and sober bearing of Cavenish. He replied less pompously:

"Yes, yes. That is true—but you see my difficulty. I am alone—my fellow-constable is ill, and I must have assistance."

"Quite so—and the best thing for you to do is to go and telephone to your headquarters, leaving your prisoner here," replied Cavenish. "You probably know the locality better than we do—we are all newcomers here—and you will get the co-operation you need more quickly if you do the explaining yourself. We shan't run away—and your captive can't run."

"It's all very irregular," said the Special, and Bruce Manaton put in:

"It's not my idea of regularity either, having murder at supper time. So far as I am concerned, the sooner you get the assistance you need, the better. I want my supper."

"Your levity is misplaced, sir. This is a serious matter," boomed the big Special, and Rosanne broke out:

"Do you think we don't realise it's serious? It's horrible—for all of us," and Ian Mackellon put in quickly,

"Look here, sir, this is just quibbling. Do you want one of us to go out and try to find a telephone, or are you going to do it yourself? As Cavenish says, you're safe enough in leaving this fellow here with the four of us to look after him, but we don't want to behave as though we were in a Russian novel, and talk about it all night."

"I will go myself and telephone—but you people must be responsible for my captive until I return," replied the big man pompously. "I must ask your names before I leave you, and—er—see your identity cards."

"The official mind at work," said Bruce Manaton softly.

CHAPTER TWO

I

T HE BIG SPECIAL CONSTABLE LEFT THEM ALONE FOR A WHILE at last. As Cavenish said afterwards, the man had done things the wrong way round—as representative of the law he should have stayed with his captive and sent one of the other men to telephone or to find a policeman, but obviously this "Special" did not trust any of the oddly assorted party to give a message properly. He wanted to do it himself. Cavenish and Mackellon both later admitted their unwillingness to go away from the studio leaving Rosanne to face the incalculable behaviour of her irritable brother, and the pompousness of the war-time representative of the law. Delaunier they discounted as a man of no ability whatever save in his own profession.

When the front door closed behind the Special, Bruce Manaton said coolly:

"Well, I'm going to have my supper no matter what happens—or what's happened." He turned to the Tommy. "Like some beer? You look frayed out."

The lad shook his head, and Rosanne said to him,

"You've hurt your ankle, haven't you? Better get your boot off before it swells."

He looked at her in a puzzled way. "You heard what that guy said?" he asked. "He told you I was a murderer."

"I know he did. I should think he's very stupid," replied Rosanne calmly. "I don't know anything about you, but if you're hurt, I'm quite prepared to bandage you up."

Cavenish came over to the lad and held out his hand to him. "I don't know anything about you either, but I'm prepared to go as far as Miss Manaton. Let's undo your boot and see the damage."

"Decent of you. It hurts like hell. I can't think why you should bother." He broke off, and then said, "Someone's bumped off the old guy upstairs—in the house up against this studio. That swollen-headed cop said I did it. I didn't. I just found him. The front door was open and I walked in. He was my uncle."

Cavenish was kneeling down untwisting the lad's puttee. He replied: "You know the best thing you can do is to keep mum and tell the whole story to the police when they ask for it. If you get talking now we shall all be questioned as to what you have said, and the result will be confusion." He began to unlace the heavy boot and the boy winced with pain, his face green.

Delaunier spoke next:

"Damn all, Cavenish, I want to hear the story. It might dramatise well. I thought so when that bleating ass of a Special came blundering in. He over-acted, of course—still, it was a good situation. Good theatre, y'know."

Cavenish had managed to get the heavy service boot from the lad's foot and was removing the sock from the bulging ankle, already swollen and puffy. The lad retorted angrily to Delaunier,

"Theatre, you call it? It may be fun for you, but for me it's ruddy hell. I came over here to fight, and now it looks as though I shall get hanged for my trouble. Oh hell! Why did I ever go inside that house? The front door was open, and I just walked in—walked into a trap... It was all dark in there, and no one answered when I shouted. I went upstairs—I knew the old man slept up there—and I found him, on his bed, with his brains blown out all over the pillow... and then that cop came in and found me, and said I'd done it. Oh, God, how can I prove I didn't do it…"

The others had all been silent during this outburst: the lad's voice was hoarse, and his words tumbled out in a rush, as though the very effort of speaking gave relief to his overburdened mind. Delaunier, still with a glass of beer in his hand, leant forward listening, for all the world as though he were critic at an audition, cool and inquisitive. Bruce Manaton had sat down at the supper table, and was eating as a hungry man eats, intent on his food. Mackellon was sitting sideways on his chair, his long legs curled round one another, his face furrowed in perplexity. Delaunier asked:

"What made you go into the house at all?—just curiosity?"

"No." The lad almost shouted in exasperation. "I tell you he was my great-uncle, my grandfather's brother. My name's Folliner, too—Neil Folliner. I wrote to him before I first came over here, and I'd been to see him before. I wrote and told him I was coming this evening, too. When I saw the front door was open I went inside. I knew something queer must have happened. You folks over here don't leave your front doors open for anyone to walk in. I went up to his room—I'd got a torch—and there he was."

Rosanne had produced a bandage and some iodine, and Cavenish was bandaging the swollen ankle with neat skilful fingers. Delaunier, still with the same cool impersonal curiosity, enquired,

"And when did our cod-faced pomposity arrive—the representative of the law as he lovingly described himself?"

"The cop? He barged in when I was standing by the bed. I was all het-up and muddled. I didn't know what to do. I'd suddenly realised what it looked like, me standing there beside that horror… It *was* horrible. Maybe I'll get used to seeing things like that when we're fighting, but I'm not used to it now. His grey hair—all in a puddle. Oh, Lord."

"No use thinking about it, laddy," said Cavenish gently, sitting back from his task, but Delaunier went on.

"When you saw the constable, what then?"

"I suppose I lost my head. He stuttered something about arresting me, and I bolted. I got past him, out of the door, and bunked downstairs. It was dark, and I fell over something in the vestibule and twisted my ankle. I got up again and found the door, and doubled back and got into the yard—but he caught me. I couldn't run. It was all up once he grabbed me. He's got beef, that chap. I gave up. I knew I couldn't get away."

The unhappy voice trailed off into silence.

Ian Mackellon said, "Rough luck," and Manaton raised his angular brows.

"Not proven," he said softly, and then asked: "Did you say the old man was stabbed?"

"No. I didn't. He'd been shot. Close range, too. No mistake there."

Manaton went on: "Had he been dead long?"

"No. Couldn't have been… You'd have known if you'd seen him. He was still—oh, heck. It was grim."

"Then why didn't we hear the shot?" demanded Delaunier. "We were all in here, and it was absolutely quiet. Did any of you hear a shot?" he demanded.

Nobody spoke, and in the silence came a loud bang on the studio door. Neil Folliner cried out "God, what's that?" and Rosanne jumped as though she had been stung.

"The representative of the law again," said Delaunier.

II

It was the Special Constable who had knocked, banging on the studio door in a manner calculated to assert his own importance. Delaunier had suggested that they should leave him to cool his heels out in the fog, but Bruce Manaton had shaken his head and gone to the door. Rosanne turned away from the look on Neil Folliner's face, a look of desperate appeal which haunted her for long afterwards.

When the door opened, the big man blustered into the studio, and his eyes rested on the Canadian with satisfaction and relief.

"Ah... I had my doubts about the wisdom of leaving the fellow here, but I see that all is well. The regular force will be here shortly, and they will relieve you of his presence." He looked around condescendingly.

"Even among such Bohemians as yourselves, it must be unusual to have an—er—murderer thrust into the company."

"Look here, Mr. Special Constable," said Bruce Manaton, "you may be within your rights in making an arrest, and even in throwing your weight about while doing it, but you are neither judge nor jury. I've no data to go upon: for all I know you may be the murderer yourself, but I warn you of this. If you can't keep a civil tongue in your head, out of that door you go, and in the fog you stay, so far as I am concerned."

The big man's face flushed a heavier red. "You dare to threaten me?" he demanded pompously.

"I'm not threatening you: I'm telling you just where you get off," replied Manaton. "This is my home, and if you can't behave like a decent human being, I won't tolerate you in it. Any flat-footed constable off the beat could teach you manners."

"Thank you for that, chum."

The Tommy spoke with a simple sincerity which relieved the tension of the situation, and Ian Mackellon found himself able to chuckle.

"The whole situation is outside my experience," he said, "but a glass of beer won't do anybody any harm. What about it?"

He turned to the Tommy, who responded with a faint grin, which gradually lightened his troubled face.

"You folks are white all through. You've been decent to me, by gum you have!" he said, as he took the glass Mackellon held out to him, and raised it to Rosanne. "Lady, here's all the best—and thank you!"

The Special Constable raised his pompous voice. "This is quite out of order: this man is under arrest, and I—"

Rosanne's quiet voice intervened: "Why behave like a Prussian bully? He may be under arrest, but nothing has been proved against him. In any case, he's hurt. Let him have his drink in peace."

The big man flushed a deep angry red, and Manaton cut in,

"You're one of the blokes who brags about Empire, I haven't a doubt, and you expect young chaps like this one to come from overseas and do your dirty fighting for you, but you can't even give him the benefit of the doubt when you find him in a mess. As I reminded you before, you're neither jury nor judge."

"You fail to realise the situation; you are behaving in a manner totally irresponsible," boomed the Special, and then another loud knock came at the door.

"That'll be the professional cops," said Delaunier. "Give me the pro. every time. Amateur performers always give me the pip."

A sergeant and a police constable came in when the door was opened to them, and blinked a little when they first came into the radius of bright light. The Special began pouring out a flood of description, but the sergeant cut him short:

"Very good—but we'd better have your statement taken at the station. There's a van outside—you can take your prisoner along and charge him before the inspector. We have to investigate in the house adjoining. I take it you sent someone in there to stand by?"

The Special shook his head. "No. I had no one to send. These people here... I didn't quite... er..."

"He probably thought we were all in it," said Delaunier, and Manaton grinned.

"That's about it, officer. The gentleman disapproves of us."

The sergeant disregarded both speakers completely, and turned to Folliner. "Now then, boy. You've got to come along. You've been cautioned, I take it? Hullo—damaged, are you? Can you walk?"

"More or less." Folliner took a tentative step forward, but it was obvious that he could only stand on his undamaged leg. The sergeant said,

"All right. You'll have to hop. Give him an arm, Macey, and we'll see him into the van."

The sergeant and constable supporting him on either side, Folliner hopped across the studio floor, calling over his shoulder to Rosanne:

"Good-bye, lady, and thank you."

"Good-bye, good luck," responded Rosanne, and Delaunier said to the Special:

"Decent fellows, our regular police. Does one good to see them, what?"

The Special turned to the door, exasperation in every line of his large but rather foolish face, and he followed the sergeant and his charge into the fog.

"Oughtn't you to stay and keep an eye on us? We're fishy, you know," called Delaunier after him.

Cavenish said good-temperedly, "Don't bait him, Delaunier. After all, he had a difficult job to do."

"Nasty bit of work," replied the actor. "Is this the curtain, think you? I'm beginning to feel hungry now the show's over. What about that stew?"

"It's stone cold," said Rosanne, and Mackellon put in:

"If you'd said curtain-raiser instead of curtain you'd have been nearer the truth, Delaunier. We shall have Scotland Yard here before the evening's out, to ask what we all know about it."

"Damn-all," replied Delaunier. "We were all of us in here together—"

"I wasn't," said Rosanne. Her words were cut short by another bang on the door.

"Oh, lord, more of them," groaned Bruce, and opened the door to the sergeant.

"Sorry to interrupt the party, sir," said the latter, civil and cheerful. "This investigation will be taken over by the C.I.D. One of the Chief Inspectors will be coming along, and he'll want statements from all of you. I thought I'd better warn you in case anyone was thinking of going home. You're not all residents here, I take it?"

"Two residents only—myself and my sister," replied Bruce Manaton. "Mr. Cavenish, Mr. Delaunier, Mr. Mackellon—meet the arm of the law proper. Do you want their addresses?"

"No. Not at the moment. I want to get busy in the house adjoining. In case there's any misapprehension, and the visitors get tired of the party, I've a man outside just to see that nobody leaves before he's said his bit."

"Right oh, sergeant! You'll find us all waiting for you. We didn't care for your friend in the Specials overmuch."

"I don't think he cared for you overmuch, either," responded the sergeant with a grin as he went out again.

"Nice chap, that," said Delaunier. "Now what about that stew?"

III

No one save Delaunier was interested in the stew. Manaton said again:

"Why didn't we hear the shot? That young chap said his uncle had been shot. Queer we didn't hear it."

"I'm not so sure about that," replied Delaunier. "Do you remember you stepped back and side-stepped into that stool there, and made a racket upsetting it. Didn't you say something about 'What the hell was that'?"

Manaton pondered: "Yes. That's true," he responded. "There *was* a thud or a bang of sorts. I thought Rosanne had come a mucker in the kitchen."

"Yes. A thud: that just about describes it," said Delaunier. "Isn't it true that fog deadens sound?"

"That's an old wives' tale," said Cavenish. "Sound travels in a fog as it does in a clear atmosphere. The thing which I find interesting is one's capacity for forgetting—or not registering. When you said that none of us heard the shot, I agreed with you. I didn't remember hearing anything. Now you mention that Manaton dropped something, I do remember having heard something outside. It was just before you took my knight's pawn, Mackellon."

"Was it? Perhaps you're right. I'd been working at that pawn for half an hour. It was your only hope, but you shouldn't have moved the bishop... Yes. Now I come to think of it, there *was* a noise of some kind."

Cavenish turned to Rosanne. "Didn't you hear anything, Miss Manaton?"

Rosanne was sitting with her chin in her hands, her elbows on the table, staring downwards.

"No. I heard nothing," she replied.

Bruce turned to her abruptly. "Weren't you in here?" he asked. "You wandered in and out, you know. I believe I cursed you, because the light from the kitchen shone across."

"What time was it when you heard the noise?" she enquired.

"Lord knows. I don't," replied Bruce. Delaunier leant forward.

"It was just before nine. I looked at my watch because I generally listen-in to the nine o'clock news, and one gets a sort of time-sense. I remember wondering why you two don't get a wireless set."

"Then I wasn't indoors at all. I went outside just before nine to look at the black-out."

"Oh, hell, what did you do that for... these ruddy police are certain to make a huroosh if you tell them that," said Bruce impatiently. "Much better say you were in here with us. You probably were. You've no idea of time, Rosanne."

"I tell you I wasn't in here, Bruce. The last time I came in here was just before Mrs. Tubbs looked in. She had been in to see if Mr. Folliner was all right. He's had 'flu, or something." She broke off, and sat staring down at the table, her finger tracing patterns on the cloth. "Rather queer: she put his door key down on the kitchen table and forgot it. It's there now."

"Good God!" exclaimed Delaunier. "Folliner's door key on *your* kitchen table. I don't like that..."

Manaton got up and made a move towards the kitchen door, and Rosanne demanded sharply,

"What are you going to do, Bruce?"

"Do? Chuck that key into the dug-out," he responded, and Cavenish said quietly,

"That's no good, Manaton. The minute you begin to tamper with evidence you ask for trouble. The only thing to do is to tell the truth."

"I tell you I don't like the truth in this instance," said Manaton. "It's all very well for you—and for Delaunier and me, so far as our own selves are concerned. We were all in here, within sight of each other, the whole evening. Rosanne wasn't in here. She was by herself in the kitchen, or else outside… looking at the black-out, and that damned key was on the kitchen table." He turned again to Rosanne, his voice gentle again: "Look here Rosa, don't be obstinate. You can save a whale of a lot of trouble by saying that you were in here with us from the very moment Mrs. Tubbs left. There are four of us here to uphold you." He turned to the others. "What about it, you fellows? Aren't all of you prepared to swear that Rosanne was in here, with us, all the time?"

Delaunier's deep voice answered instantly: "Of course. Count me in, Manaton."

After a moment Mackellon said slowly:

"All right… at least, I suppose so."

Manaton turned to Cavenish. "And you…?"

"No. Sorry, but I can't do it. I *won't* do it, because I know it's a fool's game to lie to the police," said Cavenish, his face furrowed with perplexity. He went on:

"I *know* that Rosanne had nothing to do with all this. So do you. The idea's preposterous. To try to protect her with a lie is not only a mistake in policy, it's unworthy. And I tell you this," he went on with earnest conviction. "Once the police find out—as they *would* find out—that we were lying, then Rosanne would be in very real danger."

"That's perfectly true," agreed Mackellon.

Delaunier cut in contemptuously, "How *could* they find out?"

Mackellon replied: "It's one of the most difficult things in the world for even two people to carry through a successful lie in the face of skilled interrogation: for four people, it's practically impossible. Assume that we are asked detailed questions about what happened this evening. We shan't be present when the others are being interrogated: we shall have no clue to what they say *unless* everybody sticks to the truth. If we disagree on small points—as to where Miss Manaton sat, if she moved, if she spoke—and we should inevitably disagree, because we haven't time to make up and memorise a story—then the fat is in the fire..."

"Oh, rot!" said Delaunier indignantly. He got up and moved a chair forward. "Say that Rosanne sat here, and just watched the chess players."

"Very well," replied Mackellon. "In that case, you can no longer swear that *I* was sitting at the table playing chess, nor can I swear that you were on the model's platform, because Miss Manaton would have screened our view of each other. It's only a small point, but it shows how tampering with evidence breaks down."

Rosanne's voice cut in, clear and scornful:

"Thank you all very much for your good intentions and excellent arguments. Both are unnecessary. I am *not* going to say I was in here when I was not. I'm going to say just exactly what I did and exactly where I was. If any of you try to make up stories to help me, you'll only get in a mess. You four were all in here—and you can say so. I was *not* in here—and I shall say so."

"You're perfectly right, Miss Manaton, and I admire you for it," said Cavenish quietly.

Bruce Manaton turned on him furiously.

"Damn you for a poor cur!" he cried. "You run after Rosanne, and yet you haven't the guts to tell a lie for her."

"I pay her a better compliment in knowing that it is unnecessary to tell lies for her," replied Cavenish quietly.

Just as he had finished speaking a knock sounded again on the studio door. Delaunier got up, and stood superb in his Cardinal's scarlet.

"That appears to be that," he said softly. "Every man for the truth—and the devil take the hindmost."

CHAPTER THREE

I

WHEN CHIEF INSPECTOR MACDONALD FIRST ENTERED THE Manatons' studio he received the impression of having stepped on to a stage during an interval in an operatic rehearsal. (Peter Vernon, the journalist, who had a sense of detail, later asked Macdonald "Which opera, Jock?" and the C.I.D. man replied "An opera which has never been written, with music by Berlioz, libretto by Spender or Auden, decor by Picasso, and choreography by Nijinski." "Give me a seat for the first night," grinned Vernon.)

The fog from without had seeped into the great barn-like structure: it was made visible by the powerful lights which still shone in two groups: one directed on to the now empty model's platform, illuminating the big white canvas with its masterly charcoal drawing—the Cardinal's figure blocked in in harsh unerring black lines. The painter's blue coat was flung down on the floor: the broad-brimmed Cardinal's hat was hung rakishly on the top of the Spanish chair. A lay figure sprawled in the shadow behind the easel—a picture for Picasso. In the middle of the studio the fog wraiths wavered in the shadows. Closer to Macdonald, and on his right, was a group centring around Delaunier. The latter, poised as though to take a curtain, magnificent in his scarlet, held a freshly-filled glass of beer in his hand. Bruce Manaton, who had admitted Macdonald, sat on the arm of a chair, clad in a blue pull-over and grey slacks: Mackellon and Cavenish were on either side of the chess table. Rosanne leaned against the supper table, her long-limbed slimness outlined before the gay coloured checks of a peasant-weave table cloth. Delaunier raised his glass.

"Scotland Yard, *salut!*"

"Thanks very much," said Macdonald. "I begin to understand why a gentleman in the Specials felt that this evening's experiences were a bit overwhelming."

"We didn't like him," said Delaunier gravely, "but we have nothing but praise for the deportment and behaviour of his professional colleagues, the genuine Bobby of London's greatness."

"That's all very satisfactory," said Macdonald urbanely.

Bruce Manaton spoke next: "We're not mad and we're not entirely mountebanks," he said. "If you treat us reasonably we respond. May I perform the introductions. My own name is Bruce Manaton. I am co-tenant of this studio with my sister, Rosanne. This is André Delaunier, whom you may have seen in the dramatised version of 'Richelieu.' This is Robert Cavenish—he does something at the Home Office. This is Ian Mackellon, a chemist in government employment. I believe he concocts poison gases, but he hasn't the wits to disperse fogs."

Macdonald bowed gravely to each person in turn, and then said: "I am sorry that a pleasant evening should have been spoiled by the activities of my department. I admire good portraits and I enjoy playing chess. However, my job demands that I ask each of you, separately, for your account of this evening's experiences."

"Just what we had assumed," said Manaton, "though we could give you the sum total of our experiences very briefly and unanimously in chorus or antiphon, as you prefer. I am sorry we can't offer you much in the way of a private sitting-room. There is the studio, with an open gallery above. There is also a combination kitchen-bathroom. If you wish to talk to us separately, I suggest that you take the studio, and we use the kitchen as waiting room."

"Thanks very much," said Macdonald. "You're being very helpful."

Mackellon chuckled. "He's really hoping to get the inquisition over quickly, Chief Inspector. He wants to get on with his work."

"And Mackellon wants to finish his game of chess," put in Delaunier. "Black to move and mate in six moves."

"Four," contradicted Mackellon. "With the Chief Inspector's permission, I'll move the board out of the way. I should like to finish you off some time, Cavenish."

"Don't move it," said Macdonald. "I'll see the pieces aren't disturbed. From my point of view, it's easier to get a clear view of what happened if everything is left as it was."

"I say—there hasn't been a murder in here, you know," said the painter, and Macdonald replied:

"No. I know there hasn't. I have already been in Mr. Folliner's house. Now, sir," and he addressed Manaton directly. "If you will stay in here with me, and the other members of the party will be kind enough to take my sergeant into the kitchen, I will try to get through my questions without keeping you too long."

"What you say goes, sir," said Delaunier. He led the way to the kitchen and the others followed in silence, the rearguard being the C.I.D. sergeant.

II

Bruce Manaton sat down, and said,

"You'll find that chair there is fairly reliable. I know it's not my province to ask questions, but I should dearly like to know the answer to this one. Why do you assume that I, or my sister, or my guests, know anything about this business?"

"A perfectly reasonable question which I am quite willing to answer," replied Macdonald. "I don't assume anything. It happens that the Special Constable who reported the crime in the house adjoining this one gave voice to some vague—but grave—suspicions concerning the people in this studio. You can see for yourself that it is much easier to clear away such ideas at the outset, before your party is dispersed, than it would be to do so later."

"Oh, quite." Manaton sounded mollified. "Fire away, then."

"At what time did your guests arrive this evening?"

"Delaunier has been here since six o'clock. I've been wanting to paint him in his role of Cardinal for some time, only he hates posing for any length of time. I asked Cavenish and Mackellon as a bait to bring Delaunier. He's mad on chess. The idea was that he and Cavenish should have their game later in the evening, and I intended to do some quick drawings of Mackellon. He's got a good head. He and Cavenish came in about half-past seven and settled to their game. Delaunier was posing for me, with occasional rests, from six o'clock until supper time—about 9.15. My sister was doing the cooking in the kitchen. She looked in and out of here occasionally."

"The door between studio and kitchen being open?"

"No. Only occasionally. It made a cross light. We could hear her moving about though."

"That's very clear. Now during the time you have mentioned, six o'clock to nine-fifteen, were you yourself in the studio all the while?"

"With the exception of a couple of minutes when Cavenish and Mackellon came in. We broke the sitting for a few minutes then, and chatted a bit. Then Cavenish and Mackellon settled to their game, Rosanne went into the kitchen, and I got a spot of work done. I don't know if this interests you. Mrs. Tubbs, the char who does for old Folliner, came into the kitchen to see Rosanne about half-past eight o'clock. I could hear her voice—she's a glorious old Cockney. She—Mrs. Tubbs—said she had just been in to see old Folliner."

"Thanks. That's important. You can state that from the time Mrs. Tubbs came in, until you sat down to supper, you four men were in here all the time?"

"Yes. All the time. I will show you our exact positions if you like." Manaton walked across the studio to his easel, and turned it a little, so that it was in the position it had been when he was drawing.

"I was here," he said; "I moved a few paces back or to the side— so. Delaunier was sitting on that chair on the platform. He got up once or twice, to stretch, or to warm his hands at the stove and steal a glimpse at the chess-board. Mackellon sat on the far side of the chess table—he is black. As you can see, he was in my direct line of vision. Cavenish, opposite to him, was not exactly in my focus, if you see what I mean, but I was aware of him all the time. When Rosanne opened the kitchen door the light from that room shone in my eyes, and I asked her to shut it. She came in several times and stared around. She is a bit of a painter, too, though etching is her real job. Well—there we were. Is that plain enough?"

"Admirably clear, thanks," replied Macdonald. "The four of you were in this studio, all within sight of each other, and Miss Manaton was in the kitchen, coming in and out occasionally. The next question is this. Did you hear a pistol shot?"

Manaton left the easel and came back to his chair near the stove. "To say that I heard a shot consciously so that I said to myself 'that's a gun shot,' would be inaccurate," he said. "I was working hard for once, concentrating on what I was doing, and it would have taken a near miss by a bomb to distract me. I did notice a report of some kind though, and it startled me enough to make me step back sharply and knock that stool over—the one behind the easel with my gear on it. Delaunier said 'What the devil was that?' or something like that."

"And what did you reply—or the chess players?"

Manaton laughed. "I think I said 'damn and blast you—keep your pose, can't you?'—as for the others—they were playing chess. You're a player, aren't you? You can understand that it would have taken more than slight 'noises off' to make them take their attention from their board. Also, when you come to think of it, Londoners have heard so many bangs during their recent history, that a pistol shot isn't so impressive a row as it used to be." He paused and lighted a cigarette, adding, "I daresay, subconsciously, one assesses sounds in the light of one's experiences. You know the inward reaction to a bang—'That's nothing. There was no vibration with it.' It's the vibration—the shudder of earth and fabric which means something to the initiated." He laughed and added apologetically, "You'll be thinking I'm a victim of air-raid nerves. I'm not. I'm too much of a fatalist to disturb myself, but I do admit that subconscious trick of judgment in connection with a bang—'that doesn't mean anything.' One applies it to practice gunfire without even actually formulating the thought."

"That's perfectly true," said Macdonald. "It's also very interestingly put. I suppose all Londoners who survived the winter of 1940 with nerves unimpaired, did develop what the psychologists call 'a defence mechanism'—they learned to disregard disessential bangs. I take it that *you* recalled hearing the report afterwards?"

"That's it. That youngster in khaki who was brought in here by the bloodthirsty Special blurted out his story and said that the old man upstairs had been shot."

"Just a moment," put in Macdonald. "I only want to get a bare outline at this juncture, but you might tell me briefly what the youngster said while he was here."

"Briefly it boils down to these three points: A. that he did not shoot old Folliner—the latter was already dead when Neil Folliner arrived. B. that he had sent the old man a postcard to say that he was coming this evening. C. that the Special Constable came into the bedroom only a few seconds after Neil Folliner went in—the latter having found the front door open and guessed from that that something was wrong. He also blurted out something about having come over here to fight—not to be hanged. He realised how suspicious he looked. In addition to all that he thanked my sister quite prettily for bandaging him up. He was a nice kid—we all liked him."

"Thanks. Now to get back to our discussion about the shot."

"Yes. We talked it over after the Special had gone. When we were alone we began to wonder why we hadn't heard the shot, and Delaunier recalled my knocking over the stool, and the noise outside which had preceded it. He was quite right. I remembered it then."

"Do you know what time it happened?"

"I haven't a watch, and I'm not good about time. Ask Delaunier—he can be much more explicit. I believe I'm right in saying you only want me to state my own evidence, as it were—what *I* noticed myself."

"Perfectly correct."

"Then I can't tell you the time I knocked over the stool. I can tell you that my sister brought the supper in within a few minutes of that incident, and that the Special came to our door before the supper was served out—and Rosanne isn't slow in getting a meal pushed round."

"That's all quite helpful," said Macdonald. "Now obviously I want to ask you a number of questions about Mr. Folliner—he's your landlord, isn't he?—but I don't want to keep your friends in the kitchen indefinitely. The simplest course for everybody will be for me to see Mr. Cavenish and Mr. Mackellon, and let them go home. Then your sister and you will perhaps tell me all you can about the deceased."

"Right. I tell you frankly we don't know much. He was a nasty old skinflint—and that's about all I can state with any certainty. Now would you like me to send Cavenish in?"

"Thanks very much. I'll get through the preliminaries as fast as I can."

III

As Manaton walked across the studio to the kitchen door, Macdonald reflected on his words: "We're not mad, and we're not entirely mountebanks. Treat us reasonably and we respond." The painter had shown himself to be a reasonable man and a careful witness—both more reasonable and more careful than the Special Constable who had given voice to accusations concerning the party in the studio. When Cavenish came in, Macdonald in observing him reaffirmed his original impression—here was a reliable and thoughtful man, a typical first-class Civil Servant.

"I'm afraid I've spoilt your chances of finishing your game this evening, Mr. Cavenish," said the C.I.D. man, "but I thought you might be glad to get a brief interrogation over and get home. The fog is pretty thick."

"Thanks—I shall be glad to get home, and it's going to be a bit of a job. However, Mackellon lives near me, and he's a reliable chap, fog or no fog. I'm afraid there's nothing I can tell you which is of any value."

"When did you get here this evening?"

"Seven thirty-five as near as makes no difference."

"And you settled to your game almost at once?"

"Within a quarter of an hour. Delaunier was already arrayed in his scarlet, and he soon took to his pose. You can see the positions of chess-board, chairs, easel and platform. As I sat, facing Mackellon, I was able to see Delaunier out of the corner of my eye, as it were. He made a blur of scarlet which reflected the light, and I was conscious of it even when I wasn't looking at him. Mackellon was facing the other way, so that he saw Manaton when he looked up."

"Quite—and you were all in the studio, within view of one another, from the time the game started, until the Special knocked at the door when you were beginning supper?"

"That is so. Miss Manaton looked in on us occasionally from the kitchen."

"Did you hear any report outside?"

"There was a sound like a motor backfiring shortly before supper—it would have been about five minutes to nine, I think, but I can't be exact. Manaton knocked something down, and then swore at Delaunier for losing his pose. I was preoccupied with the game and didn't take much notice—I was aware of Manaton and Delaunier, but what interested me was losing an important pawn. Mackellon diddled me properly."

Macdonald laughed. "Yes. It's queer how an experienced player can still have a blind spot. Have you known Mr. Manaton for some time?"

"Only for a few months. I have known Delaunier as a chess player for some years. He occasionally comes to my rooms for a game, and he brought Manaton with him one evening. Since then, we have had one or two good evenings in this studio, with two chess games going. Miss Manaton plays a good game. Her brother amused himself drawing the players. He has done one very fine study in oils of two chess players."

"I should like to see it some time. Now I don't want to keep you longer than necessary this evening: if further questions arise I can ask them later—is there anything you would like to volunteer in the way of a statement?"

"Only this. It has no direct bearing on the crime, but I should like to put on record that the behaviour of the Special Constable who made the arrest was overbearing and irritating. Bruce Manaton is an irritable fellow, and he probably spoke foolishly—but I couldn't help sympathising with him. Taking it by and large, I think the party in here behaved reasonably well. Miss Manaton and I bandaged young Folliner's ankle. For some reason or other, all of us felt very strongly that the lad wasn't a murderer."

"Feelings don't get a detective very far," said Macdonald. "What did Folliner tell you himself?"

"Briefly—that he had written to his uncle saying he was coming to see him this evening. When he arrived he found the front door open and went upstairs to his uncle's room; he saw the light under the door, went in, and saw the old man lying dead. A moment later the Special appeared in the room and Folliner lost his head and tried to escape. He tripped over something in the hall and twisted his ankle—and was caught a moment later. He admitted frankly that he tried to run away, saying he realised how suspicious he looked." Cavenish paused, and then said, "I couldn't help wondering how the Special appeared at that very apposite moment."

"That will be looked into," responded Macdonald. "I should be grateful if you would do one thing for me, Mr. Cavenish. When you get home will you tax your memory and try to write down accurately every word that Neil Folliner said while he was in here—in his own words. I know this won't be easy, but I think that you probably have an accurate memory—given time to recall events."

Cavenish nodded. "I'll try. I take it you don't want me to compare notes with Mackellon, for instance?"

"I'd rather that you didn't, please. I'll ask him to do the same thing—again without comparing notes with anybody."

"Right. I'll do my best alone. Do I leave the resulting composition at Scotland Yard for you?"

"Thanks very much: that would be helpful."

A few moments later Mackellon came into the studio to be interrogated in his turn. His evidence was mainly a recapitulation of that already given. He spoke tersely and clearly, pondering carefully over each statement before he made it—a shrewd and conscientious witness. Macdonald asked him, quite casually, if Rosanne Manaton had been in the studio when the sound outside startled Bruce Manaton and caused him to knock the stool over.

"No. I don't think she was, but I can't be quite certain so far as my own observation is concerned," replied Mackellon. "I was immersed in the game. I didn't really see her at all while we were playing, because the kitchen door was behind me, and I didn't look round when she came in once or twice. I was aware of her opening the door, because the light from the kitchen shone across on to Manaton when the door opened, and he complained about it. He often behaves like a boor, but there's nothing in that." He hesitated, and then went on: "If it interests you, my main recollection of the events of the evening, apart from the chess-board, is the play of colour and light around the easel. I couldn't actually see Delaunier, but the strong light caused the scarlet of his costume to reflect on to the white back of the canvas. I knew when he moved, because the reflection moved. When Miss Manaton opened the kitchen door, I knew it because the pattern of light and shade altered. When Manaton moved I was aware of it even though I wasn't watching him—that intense blue of his coat caught the light, too."

Macdonald nodded. "Yes. I see. Do you paint, too?"

Ian Mackellon laughed. "A little—but don't tell Manaton so. He's intolerant of the amateur."

IV

Delaunier gave his evidence in the manner of an actor taking the centre of the stage. He had a fine voice, but Macdonald found the deep tones slightly irritating—there was a mannered quality about Delaunier's admirable diction which made his speech seem unreal. He went and sat in the Spanish chair on the platform and talked from there.

"As a matter of fact, I can tell you more about the events of the evening in here than any of the others can," he said, "because I was the only one whose mind was not preoccupied. Cavenish and Mackellon were thinking about their game. Manaton was thinking about his drawing. Rosanne was thinking about her cooking. I had nothing to think about but the others. I could recapitulate most of the moves on the chess-board, for instance—I could see it quite clearly. For instance, when the charlady was chatting in the kitchen, Mackellon castled. A few moves later he first put his opponent's king into check and took a rook at his next move. Just when the bang occurred outside, Mackellon took his opponent's knight's pawn." He paused, and waved his fine large hand. "This narrative is pure waste of time from a detective's point of view. Four of us were in the studio—myself, in this chair, and three others who were under my observation throughout. Miss Manaton was in the kitchen the whole evening, save for four occasions when she came in here and stood at the door, and a period of two or three minutes when she went outside to inspect the black-out."

"How do you know she was in the kitchen when you could not see her?"

"My dear chap, I could hear her. My hearing is very acute. *Figurez vous, mon cher*," he continued cheerfully and expansively. "I am not an artist's model. I, André Delaunier, I am an actor. I take no pleasure in sitting like a dummy, with no lines to say, no movements to make. I bore myself here on this chair, doing a *tableau vivant*. I must notice something to occupy myself. There was the chess-board—but Cavenish is no player. He does the obvious thing every time—generally what his opponent means him to do. Bruce—he draws. I cannot see his drawing. He curses me at intervals. I must stay put, I must fix my eyes on the players. But Rosanne, she can cook, I tell you. Yes. She can cook well. I am hungry. I listen to her movements and hope for my supper. I hear her open the casserole, move a saucepan, put plates to heat. Oh, yes. I listen. A hungry man—that is I. A dummy on a chair, yes, but waiting to be fed. You follow me?"

Macdonald chuckled. "Yes. I follow you—and you never got your supper after all. It was unfortunate."

"Oh, that was immaterial. Things happened and I became interested. There was movement, action, drama. Besides—while you talked to Bruce and the others, I ate my supper in the kitchen. A pity to waste the good stew. Listen to me, Chief Inspector," and Delaunier bent forward, waving an admonitory finger. "To ask us what we do, here, in this studio, a necessary preliminary, perhaps, but a waste of time. The man you have to watch is that Special Constable, that pompous, unpleasant, *frightened* Special Constable."

"Frightened?"

"Yes, Chief Inspector, frightened. I tell you that I, as an actor, have
studied psychology. I have studied reactions to emotion—hate, joy,
sorrow, fear. That man was frightened. The young soldier, he was
afraid, too, but in a different way. He was not afraid to *show* that he
was afraid. The Special now, he covered up his fear. He blustered.
He bullied—*but* he was afraid. His hands were shaking, his eyes
bulging. Yes. I tell you he was afraid."

"He'd had rather a dramatic evening, you must remember,"
said Macdonald. "It isn't the lot of most Special Constables to
discover a crime of violence, and to follow that discovery by breaking into a studio party very far removed from the usual contacts
of a successful business man. It is probable that his overbearing
manner, to which you all took such strong exception, was a defence
mechanism to conceal the fact that he felt completely flummoxed.
Think that over, Mr. Delaunier, and see if it fits in with your reading of psychology. Meantime, many thanks for your assistance in
the matter of evidence. I hope you have not got far to go on this
foggy evening."

Delaunier smiled. "My congé, so to speak? It is time for me to
go? Frankly, I regret it. I should have been interested to stay, to assist
you in your investigation, perhaps. Come, Chief Inspector—I have
suffered all the inconveniences of this evening of crime. Let me have
a make-weight. I should like to study the actions and character of
a famous detective. It would be valuable experience for me. In my
opinion, the stage detective is always over-acted."

Macdonald laughed. "I'm sorry," he said, "but our regulations
do not allow Watsons. As a matter of fact, the routine work of
detection is no more dramatic to watch than the routine work of
an auditor at his books."

Delaunier sighed. "You disappoint me," he said. "I hate to be left out when there is anything of interest afoot. However—you ask me to go, and I go with a good grace. Good-evening, Chief Inspector." He got up, strode down from the platform, and turned back to look at Macdonald before he reached the door, striking a pose as an actor taking a curtain.

"Remember what I told you," he admonished. "There was a frightened man in this studio this evening—a man who was afraid of *showing* his fear."

As the scarlet-clad figure made its impressive exit, Macdonald felt that his own "Good-evening" had been an anti-climax, if not an impertinence.

CHAPTER FOUR

I

IN CONTRAST WITH DELAUNIER'S DRAMATIC SPEECH, ROSANNE Manaton's terse narrative seemed almost bleak. She wasted no words, and it was evident enough that she was tired of the evening's proceedings. Macdonald found as a general rule that most people enjoyed making a statement, very much in the way that bombed-out people enjoy recounting the horrific experiences through which they have passed. Rosanne's evident intention was to say what she had to say as briefly as possible. She stated curtly that Delaunier had come at six o'clock that evening, Mackellon and Cavenish at 7.30.

"I left them in the studio and got on with my cooking," she continued. "At half-past eight Mrs. Tubbs came in to bring me some herrings she had bought for me. She is a charwoman who works for Mr. Folliner. She stayed chatting for five minutes. A little while after she left I went outside to see if the studio black-out was all right. Then I came in again and dished up the dinner. I noticed that Mrs. Tubbs had left a latch-key on the kitchen table—it is still there."

Her curt voice ceased, and there was silence for a few seconds. Macdonald studied her, quite deliberately. Somehow Rosanne interested him: he judged that she had more character than any of the other occupants of the studio that evening.

Rosanne had refused the chair which Macdonald had drawn forward for her: she stood with her back to the stove, a slim taut figure, her hands thrust into the pockets of her ski-ing trousers, her eyes fixed on the chessmen. She stood very still and her face was expressionless, as unmoved as the voice which spoke so clearly and curtly—it was a beautiful voice, Macdonald noted, singularly clear and deliberate in enunciation, and very quiet.

"Your evidence holds much more of interest from a detective's point of view than does that of your brother and his friends, Miss Manaton," said Macdonald, but she replied brusquely, as though deliberately ignoring the conversational gambit.

"There is nothing of interest in it, either to you or to me, Chief Inspector. True, I went outside and walked round the studio, but I saw nothing at all, not even a chink in our own shoddy black-out. It was foggy and cold—that was all. If you are hoping for startling revelations from Mrs. Tubbs you will be disappointed. She is a kind-hearted, generous little soul, who works hard because she can't imagine any scheme of life which isn't hard work. She left Mr. Folliner's latch-key on my kitchen table: she has done it before, because she knows it is quite safe there. None of those facts which I have related have any bearing on what happened in that house."

"Perhaps not—though there are some interesting possibilities," replied Macdonald. "Can you tell me how long you were outside when you went to look at the black-out? You went out by the kitchen door, I take it?"

"Yes. I walked up the path to the further end of the studio—the window which gives so much trouble is at the end nearest the house. I turned the corner of the studio and glanced up at the top light. The black-out was adequate: good enough to save us from being fined, at any rate. That was all I wanted to know. I came back to the kitchen and got on with my work."

"You heard nothing while you were outside?"

Rosanne shrugged her shoulders wearily.

"I heard the usual sounds which I should expect to hear; the rumble of a train, the shriek of its whistle, a faint sound of music—so-called—from somebody's wireless."

"You were back in the kitchen by nine o'clock?"

"I expect so. I didn't actually look at the clock."

"Did you hear a pistol shot, or any similar report or bang?"

"I can't tell you. I was busy with pots and pans, and I only noticed what I was doing myself."

Again there was a silence, and then Macdonald went on: "When Mrs. Tubbs was talking to you, did she mention Mr. Folliner?"

"Yes. She said that the reason she went on looking after him was not for what he paid her, but because she couldn't bear to think of him all by himself, with no one going in to see if he were alive or dead."

Rosanne broke off, and then added abruptly in that clear terse voice: "To know a woman like Mrs. Tubbs is to know what real charity means, Chief Inspector. It's not a quality you find among the intellectuals of this world. Mrs. Tubbs looked after old Folliner because she was sorry for him—because he was an old horror, as she put it. She'll be sorry he's dead, just because she was kind to him."

"Yes. I know the quality you mean, Miss Manaton. I respect it as much as you do. Charity seeketh not her own, and never faileth. Did you know—'the old horror'?"

Rosanne turned at that and met his eyes, and her own sombre regard lightened to something like a smile in return to his.

"No, not really. I went in to see him once with Bruce when we were taking this studio. I have more common sense over agreements than he has, and I hoped to prevent him signing anything stupid. Old Folliner was a miser, I thought, intent on nothing but screwing the last possible penny out of other people's necessities. He would have let this place for any purpose—as a brothel or a coiner's den—if he could have got an extra penny out of it. I managed to delete the more outrageous clauses from the agreement he wanted Bruce to sign. I have never seen Mr. Folliner since—and I hope never to smell anything like his room again."

The trenchant voice ceased, and Rosanne added: "I can't tell you anything relevant, and I'm tired. If there is nothing more you want to ask, I shall be glad to get on with my washing-up."

Macdonald nodded. "Yes. I'm sorry to have had to bother you: it's hard luck that you should have been involved in this business. Incidentally, your sleeping quarters are above there, I take it?" He nodded towards the gallery.

"Yes. I sleep up there, and my brother sleeps on the divan at the end of the studio there. Do you want to use this place to-night?"

"No. Certainly not. I have got to see Mrs. Tubbs, and I might be glad if I could use your kitchen if need be."

"Just as you like. I'll leave the door to the garden open and close the one leading in here. Then you can do what you like. I'm very sure of this, Chief Inspector. The clue to this murder will not be found in my kitchen—nor with Mrs. Tubbs."

II

Macdonald left the studio, and walked round to the front of the house—25, Hollyberry Hill was its description in the directory. It was too dark and too foggy for him to get any idea of the place from the medium of eyesight, but he had a pretty clear idea of the

general lay-out. Hollyberry Hill was a street of old houses, many
of them already derelict and waiting demolition. They had been
built over a hundred years ago, square houses of early Victorian or
late Georgian design, stucco-covered and not unpleasing in appearance, with symmetrical façades and vast windows: there were dark
basement kitchens, Macdonald knew, their windows concealed
behind built-up "rockeries," and a flight of steps led to the front
door. Each house was detached, standing in a good-sized garden,
with a tradesmen's entrance at the side, and a space on either side
of the house with a path leading to the back garden. The back
garden of No. 25 was almost covered by the studio, but a narrow
space was left between the studio walls and the garden wall, and at
the far end of the garden, so Macdonald had been told, the unwise
ex-tenants of the studio had dug a "shelter," so called—a hole in
the ground which had since become half full of rain water, held
by the impermeable London clay. Macdonald remembered the
road vaguely because as a boy he had cycled all over Hampstead,
and explored its older parts. In those days—the first decade of this
century—the houses had been well-let to prosperous tenants, and
their freshly-painted surfaces and big bow windows had rather
taken his fancy.

When he left the studio, he walked by the narrow path which
led to the front of the house, using his torch to help him on his
way. A constable stood in the front garden, swinging his arms
occasionally in the endeavour to keep warm. Having recognised
Macdonald he said:

"The surgeon and camera men have left, sir. Inspectors Jenkins
and Reeves are still inside. There's no black-out in the house, barring the bedroom and kitchen, and the shutters are too far gone to
get fixed up."

"Right. I'm afraid this is a cold job for you, Tate. The fog seems to get through everything."

"It does that, sir, but I think it will be clearing in an hour or two. There's a bit of a breeze coming from the north. It's a perishing cold night, and no mistake."

"We'll see if we can raise a hot drink presently, Tate. I want you to patrol up and down this path occasionally, and listen for any sound from the studio yonder. Don't take a header in the dug-out. There's a good spot of extra static in it."

The constable laughed. "A lot of people tried that mug's game earlier on, sir, but most of 'em have had the holes filled in since then—after the A.F.S. had pumped them dry. It was the government's fault, you know, to start with. Advised people to dig trenches. If they'd been in Flanders they'd have known better. Undrained trenches, indeed."

Macdonald went up the front steps and let himself in at the door: it had been left on the latch, and once inside he flashed his torch round the spacious hall and shivered. The place was dank, cold with an even colder chill than the outside air. The paper on the walls, once "grained and varnished," hung in strips, ghostly lines of white showing where it had come unstuck from the damp walls. The house smelt of mildew, unwholesome, sour. There was worn linoleum on the floor and the stairs, its pattern long since worn off by the passing of footsteps. As he reached the turn of the stairs, Macdonald saw a line of light beneath a door, and he advanced towards this and let himself carefully into a brightly-lighted room at the back of the house.

III

Mr. Albert Folliner had used his bedroom as his sole living room, that was plain enough. There was a fireplace with hobs on either side, and on the hobs stood cooking pots. A marble-topped wash-hand stand held an old enamel basin, some paper bags, and a variety of old-fashioned crockery, chipped and discoloured. Apart from the wash-stand, which was a very large one, the room was furnished with an old-fashioned double bedstead, of black iron and brass, a vast double-fronted cupboard of early Victorian design, a very worn armchair, and a deal table. On the latter stood some dirty plates and a chipped enamel teapot.

Detective Inspector Jenkins was standing by the open wardrobe when Macdonald entered the room, and he turned with a half sigh from his task of sorting out the papers with which the cupboard was stacked.

"What you might call a fair old mess, Chief," said Jenkins, indicating the wardrobe and its contents. "I suppose we've got to go through all this stuff. Anyone might think that sorry old lunatic had left things like this on purpose, just with the idea of giving as much trouble as he could."

Jenkins was a man of fifty odd, a big powerfully-built fellow, growing stout now, his stubbly fair hair turning grey. He had a round, rubicund cheerful face, and blue eyes as guileless as a child's. There was something inherently likeable about him, and he had the gift, as Macdonald knew, of making friends easily with the most diverse people.

As he spoke, Jenkins nodded towards the bed, where the remains of Mr. Albert Folliner were shrouded from sight under a dingy sheet.

"No object in bringing the mortuary van driver out until some of this fog's cleared off," added Jenkins in parenthesis. "The thing's plain enough as far as it goes."

"Tell me what you make of it," said Macdonald, and Jenkins continued:

"Deceased was a miser, one of the real old-fashioned storybook misers. I won't say I haven't met one before—I have, though they're getting less common than they used to be. D'you remember old Simple Simon, who was always getting run-in for begging on the Embankment—£525 we found under the boards in his bedroom when he died, and another fifteen pounds odd in his filthy bedding. He died of starvation at last."

Macdonald nodded. "I remember."

"Well, this old one wasn't far off starving, I reckon. Skin and grief, as my missis says, but he must have been worth a lot of money. In there," and Jenkins nodded towards the wardrobe, "there are records of securities he's bought and sold—I reckon it will turn out he sold everything he'd got in the way of investments, and realised them as cash. There's an empty cash-box on the floor there, fallen off his bed. I'd say it was probable that he took his cash-box out every night and counted over the notes he'd got in it—true to type. Every miser does it. Then someone got wind of his habits and came in and shot him, and walked off with the contents of his cash-box. That's all plain enough."

Jenkins walked up to the bed and turned back the sheet: "Shot at close range, right between the eyes: the pistol's on the floor—an old-fashioned Colt with a heavy charge. He couldn't have shot himself very well at that angle: in any case, the cash-box is empty. Speaks for itself." He paused a moment, and then said:

"Well, there it is, Chief. What's your guess as to the way things happened?"

Macdonald stood silent for a moment. Then he said:

"The pistol was on the floor: of course we can't be certain that it was the one used for the murder until the bullet's been examined under the comparison microscope. Any fingerprints on it?"

"Smudges—someone had gloves on when they used it."

"So I would have expected—but they left the pistol here. I'd hazard a guess that the pistol belonged to deceased, and that he produced it when he realised he was going to be attacked. The attacker turned the pistol on Folliner and shot him, and then made off with the contents of the cash-box."

Jenkins nodded, replacing the sheet, and turning away.

"That's how I see it," he said.

Macdonald walked to the bedroom door and examined the door handle and jamb. There was no bolt, but an old-fashioned key was still in the keyhole. It turned easily—Macdonald put a pencil through the wide hole in the finger-piece of the key and turned it back and forth. Then, with a pair of pliers he drew the key out and examined its butt end.

"Easy enough to turn that from the outside if you'd got a good pair of long-nosed pliers," he said. "The murderer could have come upstairs, turned the key from the outside of the door and gone straight in. The probability was that the murderer then threw some missile at the old man—just enough to confuse him and render him incapable of using his pistol—and the rest followed. That's a piece of pure surmise for you. It may all have happened entirely differently."

"It may—but the evidence all goes to support your reconstruction," said Jenkins. "First, the old man had got his wardrobe door wide open and the cash-box out on his bed. So far as I can see, the room hasn't been ransacked: most of the papers in that wardrobe are in the places where they were shoved months or years ago: everything else is the same in this one respect—nothing has been moved within the last few hours. Now I'm certain of this: no miser would admit a visitor when he's got his treasures out and he's gloating over them. That's just plain common sense. The door would have been locked. I think we can take that as a certainty." Jenkins paused, and then added: "In my judgment, this room has not been searched or ransacked in any way. The old man was in bed, and he'd got his cash-box on the bed, open—the keys are still under his pillow. He wasn't expecting a visitor. Now for the discrepancy. Under that loose pile of old newspapers in the chair there was a postcard—from his nephew Neil presumably." Jenkins pointed to the mantelpiece, and Macdonald walked up to it and read the card which lay there. It had no address heading it, and the message was written in a round schoolboyish hand. "Dear Uncle. I'll come and see you on Thursday night about eight-thirty. I've got twenty-four hours' leave, and I'll come along for an hour or so. Don't you worry. I'll do what I can. Neil."

Jenkins stood with his hands in his pockets, rocking backwards and forwards on his heels slightly, as he did when he was thinking.

"Doesn't make sense now, does it?" he enquired, and chuckled a little. "Every picture tells a story," he added, "and that p.c.'s a poem. 'Don't you worry—I'll do what I can.' Looks to me as though nephew had had a long story poured out to him on a previous visit—poor old uncle starving, and all that. I'll lay any money deceased didn't let nephew from Canada know about the contents of the cash-box. Neither, to make sense of it, would nephew have sent uncle a postcard to say he was coming to see him if he'd intended to bump him off."

"No. You wouldn't think so. The only thing is that nephew was surprised by our Special... It's a pity it wasn't the usual constable on this beat this evening, Jenkins."

"Um... you'll be wanting to look into that," said Jenkins.

"Yes. I'll make one guess about this case, Jenkins. Either it's going to be obvious and easy, or it's going to be almighty difficult. *Someone* shot the old man with his own pistol: someone walked out into the fog with his pockets crammed with loot. A dirty dark night, with visibility nil: no one outside if they could help it."

"Um... Yes," grunted Jenkins. He knew just what Macdonald meant.

IV

A moment later Detective Reeves came into the room and addressed Macdonald: "They've brought Mrs. Tubbs round here, sir. Shall I bring her up?"

Macdonald nodded. "Yes. Bring her up here."

He went to the bed and smoothed the sheet neatly over its sorry occupant. He guessed that the sight of a shrouded body was no novelty to an elderly London charwoman—and as for the rest of the room, she must have known it as well as she knew her own.

"I'm sorry to have to bring you here, Mrs. Tubbs: it's a distressing business for you."

Macdonald spoke gently as he looked at the little wizened soul who came into the room, but she faced him with the indomitable courage of her kind.

"Never you mind me, sir. I seen worse things during the blitz. 'Orrors—why, you get 'ardened to 'em. I'm sorry about '*im*, though," nodding towards the bed. "'e was an 'ard-'earted old skinflint, but I looked after 'im, same as I would a child or a loony. Bless you, I've brought 'im food to keep 'im alive before now. Did 'e just pop off in 'is sleep, so to speak?"

"No. He was shot," rejoined Macdonald. He watched her keenly and saw her mouth agape with astonishment.

"Shot? '*Im*? Shot hisself, you mean?"

"Why do you suggest that? Had he ever threatened to take his own life?"

"Lor', no. 'E'd never've done that. Wanted to live to be an 'undred, 'e told me. No. But 'e'd got a pistol. A big wicked thing it was. 'E showed it me once. 'Mrs. Tubbs,' 'e said, 'if anyone ever try to attack me, I'm ready for 'em,' and I sez to 'im: 'don't you go on so silly. Who's going to attack you, and what for? You'll be doing yourself some 'arm with that there wicked thing you've got,' I told 'im. 'You go and chuck it in the 'orse pond'."

Macdonald gradually checked Mrs. Tubbs' garrulity and led her on by specific question and answer to an account of her work with Mr. Folliner, and such details as she knew concerning him. For ten years, said Mrs. Tubbs, she had "done" for him, while he had grown steadily more and more impoverished.

"Not that I believed all he told me," she said. "This house, now, it was his own—I do know that." Apparently Mr. Folliner had let off most of the rooms in his house until such time as they grew so dirty and in need of repair that no one would take them. He had refused to do any repairs or decorations, saying that he had no money to meet such expenses. The studio had been let until the bombing of 1940, when the tenants had "walked out on him," to use Mrs. Tubbs' expression. "Pore old thing, he was in a bad way then, with no money coming in at all," said Mrs. Tubbs. "I used to come along every day, though he couldn't pay me a penny. Never knew if I'd find him alive or dead. Deary me, that was a time, that was, what with the blitz and food that hard to come by. I always brought 'im a snack, I couldn't bear to think of 'im just starving slowly. When 'e let that great awful studio to Mr. Manaton, I told 'im straight 'e'd 'ave to pay me something if I was to go on coming. 'E's dirt mean: I knew that—still old folks do get queer in the 'ead, and it's no use blaming 'em. The Almighty's got some funny ways, I always did say so. Mr. Folliner, 'e was all alone in the world, none of 'is own to care for 'im."

"Have you ever heard him mention a nephew in the Canadian Army?" enquired Macdonald. He was letting Mrs. Tubbs tell her story more or less in her own way, realising that he was getting a curiously vivid picture of the old miser as portrayed by the garrulous Mrs. Tubbs.

"Oh, 'im—his nephew Neil you mean," she replied. "Yes, I've seen 'im, and a nice good fellow 'e is—great-nephew by rights. Got all worried about 'is pore old uncle starving in an 'ovel as 'e put it. Old Mr. F., 'e was cunning as well as mean, I knew that, pore old misery. 'E tried to get all 'e could out of that young chap, only I put me spoke in and said to Mr. Neil private, 'Now don't you believe all 'e says and go wasting your pay on 'im. I know you boys 'aven't got too much of the needful, and you can only be young once,' I says. 'Keep your money in your own pocket, and if so-be things is really bad, I'll let you know.' I just couldn't bear to think of that nice young chap giving 'is pay away to that ole misery. When you think 'ow they're just goin' to be killed in their thousands, same as they was at Wipers last time, well it ain't fair to spoil what days they've got left, if you take me."

"Yes. I understand," said Macdonald.

V

Gradually the C.I.D. man led Mrs. Tubbs on to the events immediately preceding Mr. Folliner's death.

"I always come in and tidy 'im up in the morning," she said. "Lookin' at this room now, it's no credit to anyone, and I know it, but it'd 'ave been a sight worse if I 'adn't done what I could. I left 'im something for 'is dinner and lighted 'is fire, though 'e fussed something sinful about paying for the coal. Then these last few months I've took to popping in last thing of an evening, so as to see 'im settled for the night. Fact was, I worried over 'im," she said. "I couldn't sleep comfortable in me own bed thinkin' 'e might 'ave fallen downstairs or something, all in the dark. I often told 'im not to go outside this room after black-out, but 'e would prowl."

"He was fairly steady on his legs then?" asked Macdonald, and she nodded.

"Yes. 'E wasn't too bad. Last winter 'e 'ad a bad turn, and couldn't get out of 'is bed for rheumatism and that, and I told 'im 'e mustn't bolt the front door no longer, in case 'e couldn't let me in when I came in the morning. 'You must give me a latch-key,' I told 'im. That was after we'd 'ad a rare old to-do when 'e was too ill to come down and open the door, and I 'ad to get the builders from number ten to put a ladder up to the bathroom window so's I could get in. After that 'e gave me a latch-key, so's I could just pop in and out, which I done regular, night and morning, same's I told you."

"And when you left him this evening, Mr. Folliner seemed quite as usual?"

"Yes. Quite bright, 'e was. I saw 'im into bed between eight o'clock and 'alf-past, and then I popped in to see Miss Manaton in the studio there. I like 'er. She's a lady, and kind and polite as anyone

I ever met, and a fair old time she has with that brother of hers. I never could abide these artists, fair old muckers they always is, and as for carrying-on, well some of 'em's not fit for a decent woman to know. Miss Manaton though, she's a real lady. I'd trust 'er any-where—and that reminds me. I left the latch-key in 'er kitchen. I remembered I'd put it down on the table, but I didn't worry. I knew I'd find it there in the morning, same's I'd done before."

"Did Mr. Folliner say anything to you about expecting his nephew to call and see him, after you'd left him this evening?"

"No, sir, not 'e. 'E wasn't expecting Mr. Neil. I know that, 'cause 'e got into bed. 'E wouldn't 've got into bed if 'e'd been expecting his nephew. 'E was particular in some ways, though you might not think it, seeing 'ow 'e lived. Mr. Folliner, 'e was a gentleman once—a scholar. 'E could write beautiful, and spoke the same as you do."

Macdonald asked, "Can you read, Mrs. Tubbs? I see you haven't got any spectacles, and most folk need glasses as they grow older."

"Yes, sir. I've got a pair from Woolworth's at 'ome—suit me per-fect. I can read all right when I've got me glasses, but not without."

"Well, there's a postcard on the mantelpiece from Mr. Folliner's nephew, Neil. I'll read it to you."

Macdonald got up and read the postcard aloud, adding: "I found this card under the newspapers in the chair there."

"Well I never! That's not like Mr. Folliner. 'E was very particular about never leaving any of 'is letters about. Suspicious, 'e was. Old folks get like that, some of 'em. I've never known 'im leave a letter about anywhere—and I'm quite sure 'e'd never 've gone to bed if 'e'd thought Mr. Neil was coming—unless 'e went queer in 'is 'ead all of a sudden. That's what it looks like. 'E must 've 'ad the card and then forgot. 'E'd 'ave told me if Mr. Neil was coming. It was an excitement for 'im when 'e first 'eard 'is nephew was over from

Canada—the grandson of his brother Frederick, Neil was. 'Per'aps 'e's a rich man,' 'e said to me. And did Mr. Neil come then, sir?"

"Yes. He came this evening, and found his uncle dead."

"Deary me! It *would've* given 'im a nasty turn, poor young man. Fancy 'im shooting 'imself after all. I'd never've thought 'e'd do it. I can't help being sorry, for all that 'e was an old 'orror, as Miss Manaton said. Poor old misery! Whatever come over 'im to do a thing like that?"

Macdonald next asked: "If any letters came for Mr. Folliner, did you bring them up to him?"

"Not me. 'E took them out of the letter-box 'is self. Always went down to the door when 'e 'eard the postman's knock. I never saw none of 'is letters except when 'e was too ill to get downstairs last winter."

"Did he have many letters, do you know?"

"'E 'ad quite a lot then—all business letters, printed ones I mean Nothing private. When Mr. Neil first wrote, my old Mr. Folliner said it was the first letter 'e'd 'ad in years—meaning private letter. We used to 'ave a very nice postman on this round—Joe Baines. I know 'is mother in Camden Town where I once lived. Mr. Folliner was very put out when Joe Baines was put on another round. We've got a postwoman now, and she's often late what with one thing and another, and Mr. Folliner didn't trust 'er. Silly, I calls it. Women's as careful as men any day, and a sight better, some of 'em."

"Can you tell me if Mr. Folliner had any friends at all, or anyone who came to see him?"

"Nobody, sir. If it 'adn't been for me, no one would ever 've come to this 'ouse. It's true Mr. Manaton came in once or twice, and his sister, when they took the studio—but they've never been in since. They didn't like 'im, and it's true 'e tried to do them. 'E was

a real proper old skinflint. The folks who had the studio before—
Stort their name was—they came in sometimes, to try and get Mr.
Folliner to do some repairs. But 'e never would. Randall Stort, that
was the name, and 'e 'ad a nasty little nosey parker living with 'im,
name of Listell or something like that. Mr. Stort, 'e made a picture
of Mr. Folliner—I saw it in the studio and it gave me the fair creeps:
painted 'im like a miser, 'e did, with 'is skinny 'ands all clutching
bank-notes. You never did see such a thing. A liberty, I called it. 'I
done 'im from memory, ma,' Mr. Stort said to me, and I turned
round on 'im. 'No familiarities from *you*, Mr. Stort,' I said, 'and if I
'ad to choose between you, I'd rather 'ave Mr. Folliner any day. At
least, 'e *was* a gentleman once, and that's more'n you'll ever be,' and
I walked out with two and sixpence owing to me and me pail and
scrubbing brush just left in the middle of the floor. 'Ma,' indeed!"

There was a brief silence: Jenkins had been busy noting down the
salient points of Mrs. Tubbs' narrative, and at length Macdonald said:

"Well, it amounts to this, Mrs. Tubbs. You left Mr. Folliner about
eight-thirty this evening. He was then in bed, was not expecting any
visitors. So far as you know he was a poor man: so poor that you
have sometimes given him food to save him from starving. The only
visitor you know he had was his nephew Neil. How often had he
been there, do you know?"

"Twice. Once last October, when 'e came after tea and left when
I did at eight o'clock. Once just before Christmas, when 'e brought
some rations in one morning—a pound of Canadian butter, some
tinned beef, chocolate, and tinned milk. They're all there still, on
the top of the wardrobe."

"When you left this evening, are you quite sure you shut the
front door?"

"Me? Certain. I shook it to see, same's I always do."

"Very good. I'm afraid we shall have to ask you to come to the mortuary to identify Mr. Folliner, when we've got him moved, Mrs. Tubbs."

"That's all right, sir. I'm not afraid. I've seen too many 'orrors in the blitz to be particular. I was going to ask you, can I look at 'im? I took care of 'im, you know, same as he was a child, and I'm sorry 'e went and did that."

"I'm afraid he's a painful sight, Mrs. Tubbs—but as you will."

The little woman went to the bed and turned back the sheet. She stood for a moment or two and then replaced the sheet methodically.

When she turned back to Macdonald there were tears running down her button of a nose.

"Poor old misery," she said. "I wouldn't 'ave 'ad 'im do it for an 'undred pounds."

And Macdonald felt that to Mrs. Tubbs "a hundred pounds" was all the gold of Ophir. She could imagine no greater wealth, and the tears she shed for her "pore old misery" were token of an affection that had been genuine.

"... seeketh not her own: is not easily provoked..." the words seemed to apply to Mrs. Tubbs.

CHAPTER FIVE

I T WAS SHORTLY BEFORE MIDNIGHT THAT MACDONALD LEFT 25, Hollyberry Hill, and found that the constable on duty had been a sound weather prophet: the fog was lifting, and a chill wind from the north was blowing fitfully. Macdonald got into his car and drove to the nearest telephone call-box, where he put through a call to Mr. Lewis Verraby, the Special Constable who had arrested Neil Folliner.

"Chief Inspector Macdonald of the Criminal Investigation Department speaking. I'm afraid it's very late to bother you to-night, Mr. Verraby, but I should be glad if you could see me for a few minutes. I have been put in charge of the Hollyberry Hill case."

"Yes, yes. Of course. By all means, come immediately, Chief Inspector. I shall be very glad to discuss the case with you. You will find my house quite easily. Haverstock Close is just off the main road, the turning beyond the traffic lights on the right-hand side as you face north: number five is at the cul-de-sac end."

"Thank you for the directions. I will be with you in a few minutes."

Macdonald always found it interesting to consider the impression made by a witness first coming in contact with the police in an official enquiry. Mr. Lewis Verraby was a Special Constable, certainly, but Macdonald intended to regard him, for the time being, simply as a witness—a non-expert witness—giving evidence of a crime. There was a curious nervous tension in the voice which spoke over the 'phone: the volubility with which Mr. Verraby had spoken, his quick and enthusiastic agreement, seemed to have a nervous quality. Macdonald remembered André Delaunier's statement, "the man was frightened." Macdonald agreed with Delaunier's statement in this—that Verraby's voice indicated nervousness.

Haverstock Close was a short cul-de-sac in which five small houses of the neo-Georgian *de luxe* type had been built, both houses and roadway probably occupying the site of some demolished mansion standing in its own garden. The fog had cleared away by the time Macdonald turned his car into the cul-de-sac, and even before he was admitted to number five, the C.I.D. man had summed up the type of house in which Mr. Verraby lived—small but luxurious, probably fitted with every modern ingenuity which the domestic architect of to-day can contrive.

The door was opened to him by Mr. Verraby, who enquired, "Chief Inspector Macdonald? Come in, come in. I'm glad the fog is clearing away. Fog is the very devil when one is on duty, as I know all too well. This room on the right, Chief Inspector. The fire is still alight. You must be chilled right through. May I take your coat…"

If the night air had been raw and penetrating in its dank chill, Macdonald thought that he preferred it on the whole to the hot airlessness of the room into which he was ushered. It was a beautiful room from the point of view of design, panelled in some fine-grained wood of silkily gleaming surface, with built-in bookcases and shelves. A piled-up fire burned merrily in a beautifully designed hob-fireplace, but Macdonald guessed that there was central heating in addition to account for the even heat of the room. The air was heavy with cigar smoke, and the smell of whisky was noticeable. Mr. Verraby's hand must have been unsteady when he poured out his drink from the square Georgian decanter. Dressed in a quilted black satin dinner jacket, Mr. Verraby looked a very prosperous gentleman indeed. Macdonald took in a great deal in one deliberate glance—the panelled room with its rich, plum-coloured damask curtains, Persian rugs, gleaming crystal and silver, deep modern armchairs—the whole a bizarre contrast to the milieu in which the case had originated, "the 'orrible 'ovel" of Mr. Albert Folliner, and the gaunt studio where the Manatons lived.

Macdonald took off his overcoat—to do so was necessary in such a temperature—and Mr. Verraby went on genially, "Whisky and soda, or a hot toddy, Chief Inspector? You must need something after your investigation in that ice-house in Hollyberry Hill."

"Thanks. I'm on duty, and we don't drink on duty, as you probably know," rejoined Macdonald. He sat down in one of Mr. Verraby's magnificent armchairs (the C.I.D. man could not deny the comfort of that *tour-de-force* of modern luxury), and without further preamble, Macdonald went on: "I have the outline of your official report, but I should be glad if you would recount the whole story in detail in your own words."

"By all means, by all means. I was on duty this evening patrolling by the new Power Station at the northern end of Hollyberry Hill. As you know, we generally—er—hunt in pairs, but my opposite number, Colonel Gratton, is laid up with 'flu, and I went on duty alone. I was due to be relieved at ten o'clock. Owing to the chilliness of the night, I covered my beat more quickly than usual. Not to put too fine a point on it, it was hellishly cold, and I suffer with my liver. I walked fast in the endeavour to keep warm. Obviously, with the fog as thick as it was between eight and nine, I couldn't see very well where I was. I knew I was in Hollyberry Hill, but that's all I did know. I realised later that I was off my beat so to speak, but in the circumstances that was nothing to be surprised at."

"Quite," murmured Macdonald, as Verraby paused, evidently expecting some comment.

"It was the foulest night I remember for years," went on Verraby, "and admittedly I was fed-up. However, to get on with the story. Shortly before nine o'clock I heard the report of a firearm of some kind—"

"One moment. Did you make a note of the exact time?"

"No. Even if I'd thought of doing so, I couldn't have. You know what it is with watches these days, you can't get one repaired under six months, and you can't buy one. My wrist-watch is broken. I had a watch on me, an old half-hunter, in my waistcoat pocket, but it isn't reliable, not to within a few minutes. In fact it isn't reliable at all. It's stopped since I came in. It's there, if you care to see it—on the mantelpiece. I wound it up this morning, but it stopped, as you see, at ten o'clock."

"Then your estimate of the time you heard the report is pure guess-work?"

"Not entirely, my dear Inspector. I have an unusually accurate sense of time—I am seldom many minutes out in an estimate. I knew the time I had come on duty. I knew that I made contact with my 'point'—a regular constable on duty in the main road—at eight-thirty. I asked him for the time. It was nine-fifteen when I entered that studio—"

"How can you be sure of that, Mr. Verraby?"

"Because there was a clock in the studio, an alarum clock on a table near the stove."

"There was, but the clock had stopped. It had probably been registering 9.15 ever since the Manatons came to the studio."

Verraby laughed, a rich deep laugh, musical and well-bred, but to Macdonald's ear it lacked the essential quality of a laugh—amusement. "Ah, you have me there, Chief Inspector: you have me there. I shall have to take refuge in the time-honoured cliché, 'to the best of my knowledge and belief' it was shortly before nine o'clock this evening that I heard a sound which I judged to be the report of a firearm. Is that in order?"

"It is. Will you answer this question very carefully. Did you immediately assume that the report was that of a firearm, or did you formulate that judgment after experiencing the later events of the evening?"

"On my soul, Chief Inspector, this is an inquisition in detail with a vengeance. You don't take much for granted, do you?"

"Nothing," rejoined Macdonald quietly. "In police work detail is too important to be taken for granted. Lest you think that I am being unduly detailed, I would like you to realise this. It is very easy to forget details. The most valuable evidence is that which is given immediately after an event, before the mind has had time to forget or to modify—to 'rationalise events,' as the psychologists say."

"Precisely, precisely. Don't imagine I'm taking this amiss. I admire your thoroughness, Chief Inspector. I only wish there were more men of your calibre in the Police Force. I speak from experience, you know. Sterling fellows, our force, but lacking in finesse—one appreciates a first-class mind when one meets it. Now, shall I carry on?—and are you sure you won't forget regulations to the extent of joining me in a drink? No? Well, I've had a heavy day, and here's how!"

Having mixed himself a whisky and soda, Mr. Verraby continued: "I heard a sound which I *immediately* judged to be the report of a firearm. I was at once on the *qui vive*. It was obvious that the report was at some little distance, and probably not in the open air. I judged that the sound came from a house somewhere away to my left and in front of me. That of course was an impression, recorded by my mind as I heard the report. I stood still for a moment and listened. I heard nothing—neither footsteps nor movement. I had my electric torch with me, and I turned its beam on to the entrance of each house as I passed."

"The fog was then very thick?"

"Damned thick. I could, however, see as far as the front doors in most cases. Those houses, you will find, have only a yard or two of front garden. As a matter of fact, the majority of the houses in that block—between Seton Avenue and Dayton Crescent—are derelict, waiting demolition. I had in mind that empty houses have not infrequently been the scene of crime. I listened carefully as I walked, but I heard nothing at all. When I reached number twenty-five the light of my torch told me that the front door was open, and I decided to go inside to investigate." Mr. Verraby paused here, and then added:

"I don't pretend to be cast in a heroic mould, Chief Inspector. I felt that it was my duty to go inside that house, but I admit that I didn't relish the prospect. On the contrary, it was very definitely repugnant to me. However, I went."

Macdonald felt that he had been offered a cue—it was up to him to congratulate Mr. Verraby on his praiseworthy sense of duty in the face of danger, but something in the man's complacency made Macdonald unsympathetic. He merely enquired:

"And then—?"

Mr. Verraby's manner became a shade less expansive.

"Oh, I went downstairs to begin with, thinking that the inmates of these houses would probably favour the basement rooms. I soon realised that these were unoccupied. Then I went upstairs. I saw a thread of light under a door, and I went to it and opened it. I saw a Tommy in khaki standing by the bed, and I saw the occupant of the bed—a ghastly sight. I took a step forward, but before I could formulate a word, the soldier swung round and succeeded in getting past me to the door. I tried to stop him, but he was a powerful fellow and I was taken by surprise. I immediately pursued him—"

"One moment. Could we get this a bit clearer? When you entered the room, the soldier was by the bed, farther from the door than yourself?"

"Yes, yes, of course. I took a couple of steps forward—a mistake on my part, as I realised almost immediately. I should have stayed by the door, but I am not experienced in these matters. The murderer immediately sprang forward—"

"If you don't mind, we won't adopt any assumptions, Mr. Verraby. There is no actual proof that the soldier was the murderer."

"No? I should have thought it self-evident. However, as you will. The soldier sprang forward, eluded my effort to stop him, and rushed out of the room, banging the door as I regained my balance. I immediately gave chase, and had the satisfaction of hearing him fall heavily in the hall. This gave me an opportunity to catch up—I was nearly at the bottom of the stairs before he reached the front door—"

"The latter was still open, I take it?"

"Yes. I had left it as I found it. I expected my man—the soldier—to take to his heels in the street, but instead he turned by the side of the house. He had hurt his ankle when he fell, and he was unable to make any real speed. When I laid hands on him, he virtually collapsed."

"Did he say anything?"

"He kept on repeating: 'I didn't do it, I didn't do it. He was dead when I found him.' I ran my hands over him to find if he had a weapon in his pockets, but I did not discover anything."

"No. I don't suppose you did," said Macdonald. "If he had had a weapon, and assuming, as you have done, that he was the murderer, I don't think you would have been able to return home here, nor yet able to tell me about the events of the evening, Mr. Verraby. It is more probable that you would have remained in the company of old Mr. Folliner until someone discovered not one corpse, but two."

Verraby's rather protuberant blue eyes goggled as he listened to the Chief Inspector's quiet voice.

"That depends," he said. "You must remember that I took the fellow completely by surprise. It so happens that I was wearing shoes with crepe rubber soles, and I moved quite silently. I was on to him before he realised that he was discovered. However, that is all rather off the point. What I *should* like to discuss with you is the direction of the fellow's get-away. He made a bee-line for that studio. I am convinced that he expected assistance there, and it is my own conviction that those artist fellows were concerned in the affair somehow. Scallywags, Chief Inspector, all of them, irresponsible scallywags, capable of anything."

"I quite understand that the studio party struck you as grotesque, Mr. Verraby, but I think you are out in your estimate of them. In addition to the painter, his model, and the painter's sister, there were two visitors, the older named Cavenish, the younger Mackellon. Cavenish is a Civil Servant, Mackellon a scientist in Government employ. Neither of the two can be described as irresponsible, nor yet as scallywags. Bruce Manaton, the painter, is an irritable fellow, perhaps what you would describe as anti-social, but he is an educated man, and not an unreasonable one, so far as I can judge. Delaunier is an actor—but all actors are not irresponsible. Hasn't it occurred to you that if your surmise were correct, they could have made some excuse which would have covered the escape of the man you had arrested?"

"Of course that occurred to me, but I didn't think they would dare to try anything of the kind. I made it abundantly clear that they would be held responsible for the safe-keeping of the man I had arrested."

"And you must admit that they discharged the responsibility. Nevertheless, Mr. Verraby, since you distrusted the studio party, I am surprised that you left your prisoner in their charge. Didn't it occur to you to send one of the party—Cavenish, for example—to telephone for you?"

Mr. Verraby's face flushed indignantly.

"I used my own judgment, Chief Inspector, and I think, as events have turned out, that I was not at fault. Manaton had already refused to telephone for me, and the others were equally unwilling. I had no compulsion, no power. There were four of them, five counting my prisoner. I did my best in difficult circumstances."

"Quite so: you couldn't do more than your best, and you had to follow your own judgment," rejoined Macdonald equably. "I should like to return to your statement about searching your prisoner. You said 'I ran my hands over him.' You were looking for a weapon, a pistol or revolver, I realise that. Did you, however, notice anything bulky in his pockets? Any parcel, or bundle of papers?"

"No. Nothing bulky. He had on an army top-coat with battle-blouse underneath. I should have realised at once if there were anything bulky in his pockets, and made it my business to remove whatever it was, when we were in the studio."

"Thanks. That is a very important point," said Macdonald, but Verraby continued, rather stiffly:

"I have realised since that I made a mistake in leaving the man in the studio as I did, because it gave him the opportunity of destroying evidence. There might have been some papers in his pockets. I can put it on record, however, that there was nothing bulky."

"Very good. My next question is a necessary formality. Deceased was an old man named Albert Folliner. He had lived at 25, Hollyberry Hill for many years. Have you ever known him or had any dealings with him?"

Mr. Verraby's sanguine face again became uncomfortably suffused with red. Macdonald guessed the answer before it came, and was genuinely surprised as he realised the truth while his witness stuttered and hesitated.

"Well, the fact is, and it's a very surprising fact, though the world is a small place as we all know, er... I didn't actually *know* Folliner. In fact I should be quite justified in saying that I didn't know him at all, but I once had some business dealings with a man of that name. I have done a little speculating in property in this district: I am the owner of these little houses here in Haverstock Close. I commissioned an architect to build them after I had bought the site. Er... I bought a property which belonged to a Mr. Albert Folliner, a small property. That would have been shortly before the war. I remember the transaction particularly because he asked to be paid in cash—a peculiar request. Of course there was no question of my *recognising* deceased: apart from anything else, he was too much disfigured—but I remember the name Albert Folliner."

"Have you had any dealings with him since that date?"

"No. No... It was just a question of some small house property, nothing of any importance. He owned a small piece of land which impinged on some property I intended to develop." Mr. Verraby paused, and he smiled at Macdonald—but it was an uneasy smile.

"I'm afraid that I'm wasting your time with these trivial details, Chief Inspector. I realise that they have no bearing on the case at all, but I preferred to answer your question fully, to be absolutely frank. I should have felt very uncomfortable if you had ever reason to say to me, 'Why did you not tell me that you had heard of the man before?'"

"I quite agree with you: frankness is advisable in a case of this kind," rejoined Macdonald. "I should be interested to hear further details of your transactions with Mr. Folliner," he went on. "Was the property in question situated in this district?"

"Yes. To be exact it was in Hollyberry Hill. A small house near the main road."

"Did you find Mr. Folliner a difficult person to make terms with—did he, for instance, put a high value on his own property?"

"To begin with, the price he asked was quite fantastic: we broke off negotiations with him several times. Eventually he accepted an offer on valuation, after having tried, quite unsuccessfully, to sell his property elsewhere."

"And you paid in cash?"

"I did: he was paid in £50 notes. He refused to accept a cheque."

"A curious transaction." Macdonald's voice was quietly conversational. He went on:

"I notice that a considerable number of old houses in the Hollyberry Hill district are derelict, awaiting the housebreaker. I suppose that when they are demolished, the land on which they stand will be 'developed' as the saying is."

"Flats," said Mr. Verraby. "Good small modern flats, centrally-heated, labour saving in every way. If you build good flats you can't go wrong. The demand is unlimited. The woman of to-day doesn't want to be bothered with housework and cooking—the kitchen-range and copper régime is gone for good. Give them good small flats, with a restaurant on the premises, and service obtainable, and you can let every flat in the block before the builders are out. Of course, there's a limited demand for small first-class houses like this one, architect-built and decorated, but take it from me, the future is in flats—what with taxation and cost of living there aren't many people can afford what I call a decent house."

"You're evidently very much interested in your occupation," said Macdonald, and Verraby replied:

"Oh, I'm interested all right—from the beginning to the end. To build a block of first-class flats needs capital. I'm interested in that; capital's a very absorbing subject. Then there's the matter of choosing an architect, and putting the right type of block in the right neighbourhood, considering such details as transport facilities and shopping facilities. When I first came into the land-development business I regarded it as an amusing side-line. Now I find it's an absorbing interest—or more accurately, it *was* an absorbing interest, until this infernal war upset everything."

"Yes. It must have put a stop to your building schemes rather abruptly. It must be an exasperating situation to own a piece of land ready for development and not to be able to put it to any use."

Verraby made a wry face. "You've hit the nail on the head. Exasperating? I tell you it's maddening. Capital tied up, in many cases interest to be paid—and the whole thing's at a standstill. It's a case of survival value again; the man who manages to survive and keep out of the bankruptcy court until peace is signed is going to be in a privileged position afterwards, if he's got the land to get busy on. What's going to be the first demand when this war's over? House room. I tell you the demand's incalculable."

Macdonald got up out of the big chair.

"Well, Mr. Verraby, there may be other questions to bother you with later, but I've kept you up quite long enough for to-night. I apologise for the lateness of this call."

"Oh, don't do that. I'm never an early-to-bed fellow. Do some of my best thinking in the small hours. Don't go yet. I hoped you'd tell me if you'd come to any conclusions yet, and what you made of that precious set-out in the studio."

"I've come to no conclusions at all, but I've collected some quite valuable data. Now I've got a report to write, so I must be off. Goodnight, Mr. Verraby. Thank you for your frankness. If anything else occurs to you that you can tell me about Mr. Folliner, I shall be very much interested to hear it."

CHAPTER SIX

I

MACDONALD WENT TO SEE NEIL FOLLINER EARLY THE FOL-lowing morning. The C.I.D. man began by explaining the position to him from the point of view of the English legal system.

"I want you to understand our procedure over here before I ask you any questions at all," he said. "The man who arrested you was a Special Constable, and he acted within his powers, according to his own discretion. This Special Constable gave evidence that he had discovered a crime of violence which he assumed to be murder. He found you at the scene of the crime, and he arrested you on suspicion of being involved in it. Without going into the evidence at the moment, I think it's not unfair to say that he had grounds to justify his action. No, wait a moment," as young Folliner protested vigorously: "let me finish what I have got to say. Since you have been arrested and charged, you will appear before a magistrate: that is according to English law."

A grin spread over Neil Folliner's tanned face at this juncture. "I get you. Habeas Corpus. We had a guy lecturing to us about that. I didn't reckon to try it out myself so quickly."

"Oh, good. You know all that—well, it's a fair system to my mind," said Macdonald, "a long sight fairer than most systems prevailing on the Continent, say, at the present time. The magistrate, as you probably know, has power to release you if he considers the evidence against you is mistaken or inadequate: he has power to remand you, or to let you out on bail. It's up to him. Now for my part. I am an officer of the Criminal Investigation Department, and it is my job to investigate this crime. I want to get at the truth of the matter—that and nothing else. I am going to question you, and if, as you say, you are not guilty, it is to your own interest to answer questions as fully and accurately as you can. As you probably know, it is my duty to warn you that anything you say can be taken down in writing—"

"And used in evidence against me," quoted Folliner. "I know the patter. Now see here. I don't know anything more about this murder than you do—a darned sight less, I reckon. I'm willing to answer any questions you like. You look a straight guy to me, and that's good enough. Get on with it, and take it all down, just as you say. I got nothing to lose by coming clean, because I'm not in it, see? I know I did a fool trick trying to bolt, but I'm not a gangster, used to facing it out. I lost my head because I was frightened. Got that?"

"Yes. I follow. Now say if you start at the beginning, and tell me how you first heard of Great-uncle Albert."

"O.K. My folks have got a ranch in the Okanagan, B.C. Fruit farming. When I knew I was coming overseas, Pops says to me, 'I don't know where you're going, son, but if you land up in London, you go and see old man Folliner. He was my dad's brother, and I'd like to hear news of him. Maybe he's under the daisies. Maybe not, but I've got an address from my old dad's letters, and if you find him alive, and he's flush, maybe he'll be a friend to you.' Wal, I did come to England, and after a bit I was stationed near Aldershot, and when I got leave I came up to London and went to the address Pops gave me."

"When was that?"

"Way back last fall. End of September."

"Right. And then?"

"And then? I went and knocked at that durned front door, and the oldest guy in the world opened it. Poor old blighter! He'd got Methuselah beaten hollow. It took a lot of talking to make him tumble to who I was, and then, oh cripes, I was sorter sorry for him. I could have laughed over my dad saying he'd be a friend to me. I tell you he was next-door to starving, and not ashamed to say so. I did what I could for him. You given that house the once-over?"

Macdonald nodded.

"Well then. You know. I wrote home to Pops and told him to bung some food parcels over next mail. The only good point in the whole crazy bag of tricks he called his home was the hired woman, an old Jane named Mrs. Tubbs. She's white, she is: kept him alive out of goodness. Somehow the old guy seemed to cotton on to me, and I went there a coupla' times before Christmas. I got forty-eight hours' leave yesterday, and I mailed him a card saying I was coming. That fog of yours nearly turned me back—I wish it had—but I knew the way from the Tube up at Hampstead and I plugged on. The kid I was with tried to stop me coming, but I didn't want to let the old man down. There it was—and here am I."

Macdonald nodded. "That's all clear enough. Who was 'the kid' you mentioned?"

"Oh, can that! I don't want to get her mixed up with you cops. She's the sister of a chap I know. Never mind that."

"What time did you set out, and from where?"

"Wal, I had tea at a big joint near Piccadilly Circus—'Corner Houses' you call them, for no reason I can see—and we sat on there until nearly seven, and then we went and had one at a joint up the road. I left there about half-past seven, and got mixed up in the fog. Never thought I could get lost like that, but I did. It was after eight before I made the Tube, and it took me half an hour before I got to

Hampstead. I was being careful then: I asked the way of everyone I met; I tell you there weren't many out in the streets last night."

"Can you remember anyone you spoke to?"

"There was a Sapper I spoke to—I turned my torch on him. He was at the end of Hollyberry Hill, waiting for his Jane. I thought he must be bats to hang around on a night like that, but he didn't seem to mind. It was just after nine I got to uncle's."

"Did you hear any report or gun shot?"

"I heard lots of pops. The railway was letting off fog signals somewhere, I reckon. When I got to the front door I found it was open. Not wide open, but just standing ajar. I didn't like the look of it. I knew the old 'un wouldn't leave his front door open. I shouted when I got inside, but no one answered, and I just went on upstairs. I'd got a torch and I knew where he slept. The light was on in his bedroom—I saw it under the door. I just went right in, and saw him. It was horrible."

"What did you do?"

"Do? Nix. I was just flummoxed, as though I'd been winded. I can only remember saying to myself, 'Poor old guy, it's a dirty shame.' I just stood there, staring like a zany, and the next thing I knew was the guy in dark blue was behind me, shouting at me—"

"Behind you?"

"Sure. I'd taken about three steps into the room, and I was standing by the foot of the bed. I didn't hear him come in."

"Could the Special Constable have been in the room before you—standing behind the door?"

"Cripes! I've been thinking of that. I don't know. I tell you I don't know. I opened the door and went right in. I didn't notice anything but poor old Methuselah, until the big guy started shouting at me. He pawed me, and I shoved him off. I realised what I looked like, and I made a lunge for the door and got outside and slammed the door-to. I ran downstairs, and somehow I slipped on the floor in the vestibule—the lino was all rotten and I reckon it tripped me up. I still thought I could get away, and I turned to the back of the house, thinking I could slip away between the wall and the side of that studio. I knew I couldn't run far, the street was no good. Anyway he caught me. I was going to hit him, when I suddenly thought I was being a fool and only making things worse. I could have killed him with my hands if I'd been a killer, but I'm not, see? Rather than that, I gave in. The cop, he banged on the studio door, and they let us in. It was a rum set-to, and no mistake. I thought I was dreaming, but they were decent to me, same as your regulation cops were. Not like that old turkey—Special, or whatever you call him."

Neil Folliner paused here, but before Macdonald spoke, the lad went on:

"Now you listen to me a bit. I've had a few hours to get cool in the head and think this out, and I tell you I didn't sleep much last night. First of all, if I'd planned to shoot the old man, I shouldn't have sent him a postcard in advance saying I was coming, should I? You may think I'm pretty green, but I've got more horse-sense than that. Next, if I was going to shoot him, I shouldn't have left that front door open for anyone to walk upstairs and catch me at it. That bit don't make any sorter sense to me. I'd have shut that door and planned to get away some other how. Last, if I'd done the shooting, and got a gun in my hand, I shouldn't have let that qualified Special cop me so easy. Shoot once, shoot twice. Why not? Second time's easier and you've only got one neck to hang by. You still hang 'em in this country, don't you?"

There was fear in the lad's eyes despite his resolute voice, and Macdonald replied: "Yes. A murderer found guilty may be hanged, but not before he's had a fair trial and conclusive evidence proved against him—conclusive from the jury's point of view, that is. Quite honestly, it's my opinion that an innocent man has very little to fear in an English Court of Law. I have been instrumental in getting murderers sentenced, but I have never, to my knowledge, seen an innocent man sentenced."

Folliner grinned: a rueful grin, still half afraid, but his tired face lightened as he replied: "You sorter do me good. You talk sense, and you listen to what I say. Can I go on a bit?"

"You can."

"I said just now that if I'd been doing the shooting, I shouldn't have left that front door open for someone to come in and catch me at it. That wouldn't have suited me at all—but it might have come in handy for someone else. Shoot the old guy, and then wait for some poor boob to butt in and arrest him for murder. I can see that. What I can't see is the object of the shooting. It seems just plum crazy. The old man was just a harmless old boob, poor as a down-at-heels hobo. He couldn't have done any harm, far as I can see."

"That's my province," said Macdonald, "and I'd advise you not to think out accusations against anyone else. Better stick to plain facts for the moment. You can have a lawyer if you want one, and he'll do the thinking for you."

"That's all nice and plain, but I reckon this is a frame-up. It wasn't just chance I walked in on the old man's corpse and got copped before I'd time to think. I'm the cat that burns its paws on someone else's chestnuts, and I don't like it. You see, I didn't do it."

He spoke with a pained earnestness, and Macdonald went on:

"Then it's up to me to find out who did. Answer this next question carefully. How many people did you tell that you were going to see your uncle last evening?"

"I told my mate in camp, Joe Saunders. He came over in the same transport with me. I told the kid I went to the flicks with, and her brother. He came with us—but I didn't tell them till I saw 'em yesterday forenoon, so they make no difference. The only other person who would have known was Mrs. Tubbs. Uncle would have told her, not that that makes any difference. She's all right."

"Next, do you know the studio people at all? Have you ever spoken to any of them?"

"I don't know them. I've seen the lady once or twice, going in or out of the studio. I thought she was just fine, a real looker, but I've never spoken to her."

"Do you know anybody else in the district?"

"Barring the hired woman, no one at all. How should I?"

"When did you send the postcard to your uncle?"

"Day before yesterday. I figured out he'd get it yesterday morning."

"Do you possess a revolver or pistol?"

"None. Never had one. I've got a shotgun and a rifle of my own way back home, but we'd no use for fancy firearms. We're decent folk where I come from."

"I want you to think again about going into that house in Hollyberry Hill. You found the door open, and you say that you guessed something was wrong. You would have been on the alert when you went into the house. Did you hear anything at all?"

"Nix. It was dead quiet. I shouted once, 'You there, uncle?' I knew there was no black-out, and I used my torch, but I didn't see anything."

"Did you turn your torch light down on to the stairs?"

"Yes."

"Did you see any footsteps? The pavements were wet with the fog."

"No. I never noticed. Everything was damp, clammy."

"When you went into the room, how far did you go in?"

"About three steps, I reckon. Then I stood still. I didn't wander about any. Say, it's lino on that floor. Did you get your cameramen on to it?"

"We did." Macdonald chuckled. "We know our stuff, you know, even though we are more conservative than the transatlantic police. Well, that's all for now. When you're questioned in court, stick to your facts and don't give any opinions. That's the best advice I can give you."

II

Later in the same day Chief Inspector Macdonald was called into the Assistant Commissioner's office to discuss the case of the Hampstead murder. Colonel Wragley always enjoyed hearing Macdonald expound, though the natures of the two men frequently resulted in conflicting views based on identical evidence. Biologists pour cold water on "racial peculiarities," holding that such arguments are frequently inexact and unscientific, but the fact that Wragley was a Saxon and Macdonald of Highland Scots' extraction accounted for many of their differences. The Assistant Commissioner was white-haired now, but he had been fair-headed in his youth: his skin tanned to a brick red in sunlight, and his head was round rather than long. His sanguine complexion and blue eyes were those of an impetuous man, to whom patience was an effort requiring self-discipline. Macdonald was dark-headed and grey eyed, long and lean and built for endurance. He had a noticeably long head and the type of skin which tans slowly without scorching, and patience was his long suit.

Seeing the two men seated, the Saxon prone to sudden movement and abrupt gesture, the Scot very still, given to no gesture at all, an onlooker could have made a shrewd guess as to their qualities.

"Well, what do you make of it?" demanded the Assistant Commissioner.

"Murder by person or persons unknown, sir," replied Macdonald. "In one respect the case should be simple, but it isn't. It's one of those cases in which suspicion can be limited to a given number of persons, and each of those persons has been interrogated. The murder occurred round about nine o'clock—not long before and certainly not long afterwards. As you know, it was a foggy evening, a beast of an evening, when very few people were out of doors if they could avoid it. Now at one end of the block in Hollyberry Hill where number 25 is situated, there was a night watchman. The Electricity Company is doing some essential work there, and this man was left in charge of the electricians' equipment. His name is Bardon, and he has a good character: he has been employed by the company for years. At the other end of the same block in Hollyberry Hill, at the corner of Seton Avenue, Private William Brown of the Royal Engineers was waiting for his girl friend. He waited for one hour and ten minutes before she came to keep her appointment. It's nice to know that such constancy exists. It must be rare these days."

"Possibly, possibly. Has this—er—romance anything to do with the case?"

"Yes, sir, I think it has," replied Macdonald placidly. "Private Brown was able to tell me exactly how many people passed him during his vigil. Further, he was able to tell me who those people were, having observed them either by the light of his own torch, or of the torches the pedestrians carried themselves. Just after he reached his trysting place, Private Brown heard footsteps and a voice singing 'Tipperary.' He knew the singer—it was an elderly charlady called Mrs. Tubbs whom he had often noticed at the same spot and the same hour on other evenings. She sings when the weather's bad to keep her spirits up."

"Really. I begin to see the point, but could you expedite the narrative?" demanded Colonel Wragley.

"By all means. Brown's evidence amounts to this. During the time he was waiting, only three people passed him. One was Mrs. Tubbs, who walked towards number 25 at five minutes past eight, and returned again at eight thirty-five. The second was a special constable, identified as Mr. Lewis Verraby, who challenged Brown as to his business—and was told to mind his own. The third was Private Folliner, who passed Brown at five minutes to nine, and enquired if he were in Hollyberry Hill. Now to turn to the night watchman at the Dayton Crescent end of the block. He testifies that only one person passed him between eight o'clock and nine-fifteen. He knew the time, because there is a chiming clock on the church tower further up the road. The only person who passed him was a special constable, who walked northwards shortly after eight, and returned, walking in the direction of number 25, at ten minutes to nine. So much for pedestrians. Now the block between Seton Avenue and Dayton Crescent has only eight houses on the east side, where number 25 stands, and of those eight houses only 25 is occupied. The others are empty, awaiting demolition. Their garden gates are fastened up, and investigation shows no sign of anybody having used the gardens as a hiding-place. There were no footmarks at all, though the ground is very soft."

"Well, well. Your department seems to have done a spot of work, Macdonald."

"Yes, sir. What we call 'routine' has kept us pretty busy to-day. Now for the other side of the road. There are seven occupied houses in the same length of Hollyberry Hill. Three of these are used as a hostel for University students, girls. The remaining four houses are occupied by families. I think we can accept the evidence of the occupants that everybody living in these houses was within doors during the time in question."

"I see," said Colonel Wragley, nodding energetically. "To put matters in a nutshell, you assume that one of those three pedestrians must have committed the murder?"

"No, sir. It's not quite so limited as that. There were the occupants of the studio—"

"Each of whom has an unbreakable alibi, except the woman, Rosanne Manaton—an outlandish name," barked Wragley. "Incidentally, what did you make of these people?"

"The two chess players, Cavenish and Mackellon, seemed to be reliable and responsible persons: Cavenish has been at the Home Office for years, and is regarded as a man of high character, able and trustworthy. Mackellon is a first-class chemist, a brilliant fellow in his own line, though admittedly a man of violent temper on occasion. The painter, Bruce Manaton, struck me as a much more reasonable fellow than his appearance would lead you to expect. I remember him saying: 'We're not entirely mountebanks; treat us reasonably and we respond'—a claim which he substantiated in the manner he gave his evidence. He is undoubtedly a very able painter and a first-class draughtsman. He and his sister have been badly hit by the war, as other artists have been. The actor, Delaunier, is probably the least stable of the four men, but, just because he *is* an actor, he is difficult to assess. He is always acting."

"But since he was posing for his portrait when the murder took place, his qualities are not really of importance to us," said Wragley. "What about Miss Manaton?"

"I find it difficult to formulate any judgment about her," said Macdonald. "She gives an impression of being competent, and is certainly intelligent. I should think she finds life difficult, but she is a very reticent individual, and gives nothing away."

"And she was, by her own admission, outside in the black-out somewhere between 8.35 and 9 o'clock—and yet she did not hear a shot fired?" enquired Wragley.

"I think the sound of the shot is going to be of no value save as a nuisance value," replied Macdonald. "Owing to the fog, the railways were using the usual detonating signals, and I think it will be impossible to decide when the shot was heard. Possibly Miss Manaton was indoors again before the shot was fired. The room where the murder occurred had shutters over the windows, and heavy curtains in addition."

"Yet the shot was heard in the studio, where all the windows were shut, with frames fixed over them?"

"Possibly," said Macdonald. "Possibly not. However, to get back to more concrete facts, it seems plain that four people at least—two men and two women—could have approached number 25 Hollyberry Hill at the time in question. The two women both had means of access to the house—a latch-key. Of the two men, young Folliner had been at the house before, and could have obtained a mould of the door-key; that matter is being gone into. Mr. Verraby probably knew—what any intelligent person can observe—that the lock on number twenty-five is an old-fashioned lock with a barrel key. It is very easy to open such doors if you try a selection of similar keys on them: the variations are very slight. Mr. Verraby, having bought a number of old houses in the district, doubtless came into possession of their latch-keys."

"And—motive, Macdonald, motive?" enquired Colonel Wragley.

"In every case—profit. There is a probability, so strong as to be nearly a certainty, that deceased, having realised his landed property for cash, had a very large sum of money in his room, which is no longer there."

The Assistant Commissioner intervened here: "That motive is always a cogent one, but would it apply strongly in the case of Mr. Verraby, who is a man of substance, I gather."

"Verraby is a speculator to some extent, a speculator in land values. Before the war he made a lot of money: to-day he is not very happily situated. Most of his capital is tied up in land which cannot be 'developed,' to use the current jargon, until building restrictions are removed. I should not be at all surprised if it turns out that he is short of ready money. I know that certain big groups of speculators are trying to buy up blocks of land for later development, and Verraby, of course, could dispose of his holdings in this way; *but*— and here I am in the realm of surmise—I have an idea that he is the owner of the block of property in Hollyberry Hill between Seton Avenue and Dayton Crescent, saving only number 25, Hollyberry Hill, owned by Mr. Folliner."

Colonel Wragley gave a whistle. "By Jove, Macdonald, I begin to follow your reasoning. Naboth's Vineyard, eh? Mr. Verraby could dispose of his property for ready money if he could buy number 25, but not without it."

"That is my idea, sir, but I haven't yet got all the facts to support it. I have one very important piece of evidence which goes to prove that Mr. Verraby was not speaking the exact truth. The photographers took very careful shots of the floor in number twenty-five, in order to get all possible evidence from footprints. While many of the exposures are useless—the prints too blurred to have any value—we have two photographs which go to show that Mr. Verraby entered the house *before* Neil Folliner did, and not afterwards."

"Good Gad, Macdonald, isn't that conclusive evidence? If the fellow is lying, he's given himself away."

"He has given himself the lie, sir—but that does not prove that he committed the murder. It is still possible that Verraby found the front door open, as he said, and went upstairs and discovered the dead man, and then concealed himself when he heard Neil Folliner come into the house."

"But, *why*, Macdonald, *why*?"

"Because he was afraid, sir," replied Macdonald. "As Delaunier observed, the Special Constable was *afraid*."

"If he was afraid, the probability is that he had something to be afraid of," said Colonel Wragley. "One other point seems to arise— this matter of the faithful Private Brown. You say that he admits having stood at the corner of Hollyberry Hill and Dayton Crescent for an hour, and that he has been there frequently before. Isn't there a chance that Brown might be involved? What proof have you that he did not enter number 25?"

"No absolute proof, sir. We have studied the footmarks inside and outside number 25 very carefully, with the aid of the photographer's records, and the local men were very careful when they entered the house. Brown has very large feet, but we can find no trace of them in the house or garden. However, neither Brown nor his girl friend has been omitted from the investigation."

Wragley smiled. "You don't miss much, Macdonald, do you? Well, carry on, and report progress to-morrow. My own fancy veers towards the speculating Mr. Verraby."

CHAPTER SEVEN

I

IN A CASE SUCH AS MACDONALD WAS HANDLING NOW, TIME WAS a factor to be reckoned with in more senses than one. He realised that it would be all too easy to prove a case and get a Coroner's verdict on circumstantial evidence alone. If Neil Folliner were brought before a Coroner's jury, the bald facts of his arrest in the murdered man's room would be enough to produce a verdict which would commit him for trial as a murderer. There was motive, means and opportunity: for his defence he had nothing but the bare statement "I didn't do it." On the other hand, if the evidence against Mr. Lewis Verraby were hastily collated and similarly put forward, a similar verdict might be given in his case. Each was obvious, on its own merits—or demerits.

Macdonald wanted time—time to investigate every possibility fully. It always seemed to him that the stigma of the pronouncement "guilty" on the part of a Coroner's jury was a thing to be avoided when there was any doubt at all. The procedure which he preferred—and which he hoped to follow—was this. Folliner, having been charged, was in the hands of the civil police, and, like any other person he would appear at the inquest, fixed for the following morning. (The murder had been committed on the evening of Monday, January 20th. The inquest was fixed for the morning of Wednesday, January 22nd.) At the inquest, Macdonald hoped for a brief sitting, in which the formalities of deceased's identification, discovery and place of death should be stated by witnesses as the law required, and then an immediate adjournment, "pending the production of further evidence."

Fortunately, the Coroner of the London district where the inquest would be held was an experienced and able man, who understood the desirability of co-operating with the police and not embarrassing them, as it was possible for an inexperienced or self-seeking Coroner to do. Furthermore, the present practitioner was a man who "would prevent his witnesses making fools of themselves," as Jenkins had once put it. Macdonald guessed that Mr. Lewis Verraby, for instance, would be very firmly dealt with if he tried donning the mantles of both judge and jury in the Coroner's Court. One retired Coroner of the Metropolitan Courts had once told Macdonald that he considered the main function of his office was to control the imbecilities inherent in human nature. "You always get at least one idiot on a jury—generally the sort of fellow who wants to draw attention to himself by asking unnecessary questions, and as for witnesses, it takes the patience of Job to keep them to the point and prevent them repeating hearsay as fact."

Having arranged the time of the inquest and made such suggestions as to the calling of witnesses which came within his province, Macdonald had organised his further investigations. Inspector Jenkins was left to the task he had begun: that of going through the papers in Mr. Albert Folliner's room. Inspector Ward was entrusted with the task of preliminary enquiries into the transactions of Mr. Lewis Verraby. Ward was one of the Hendon-trained officers of the C.I.D., still a youngster, and a very able one. A motoring accident which had left him slightly lame had prevented him joining-up with the armed forces, as some of his fellows had obtained permission to do. Ward was a lawyer's son, and he had just the needful qualities to enable him to make the necessary enquiries about Verraby without doing that gentleman the injustice of prejudicing his position in the eyes of his business associates.

For the moment Macdonald himself wanted to concentrate on number 25, Hollyberry Hill, the studio, and immediate surroundings. The "obvious" channels were all being investigated. The Chief Inspector had a few ideas of his own concerning less obvious ones. Characteristically, Macdonald set down all evidence very fully in his official report, but he did not (sometimes to Colonel Wragley's annoyance) consider it incumbent on him to set out all his own ideas until he had either "exploded or confirmed them," to use his own phrase.

II

Detective Reeves had been given a number of small jobs to do in connection with the Folliner case, and he entered into them all with the enthusiasm which made him such a valuable member of the C.I.D. Reeves was only thirty years of age, and if he had had his way, he would have been expending his enthusiasm in the R.A.F., but the authorities considered that as a trained and expert detective, he was of more value in the C.I.D. Reeves had complained bitterly to Macdonald that he wanted to "have a crack at 'em"—meaning the enemy; "you've let all the beefy young idiots go, and I have to stick on here at the same old grind," said Reeves.

Macdonald nodded. "So do I, you're not the only chap who'd like to be somewhere else," replied the Chief Inspector.

Macdonald had always liked Reeves, valuing his capacity for hard work, his Cockney wit and courage, but during the winter of 1940 a closer bond had tied the two men together. They had worked with the Rescue Squads when London was raided night after night, and had survived dangers and witnessed horrors unforgettable. There was no risk which Reeves would not take, but he used his wits all the time, and his wits saved many lives, as Macdonald had cause to know.

One of Reeves' first jobs was to visit the A.R.P. headquarters for the Hollyberry Hill district, and to see the Head Warden.

"Have you had any trouble with inefficient black-out at number 25 or at the studio there?" he enquired.

"Not just recently, but a lot earlier on," replied the warden. "The previous tenants of the studio were a tiresome lot, and I had to have them summonsed. However they packed up in August '41, and the studio was vacant until three months ago. Miss Manaton is a sensible woman—she's a lady, too—and I knew she was doing her best. It took a bit of fixing up to get that north light properly blacked out, it was necessary to paint six inches all round the glass, as the curtains never fitted properly, and even when they got a frame fitted up it showed chinks. Manaton himself is a tiresome customer—wanted to keep his blessed top-light clear, but his sister took no end of trouble over it. She made him get the glass blacked at the edges eventually, and she undertook to go out and inspect herself every night. I haven't had any complaints since then. As for Number 25, it was no end of a picnic. It took the old man some time to get it into his head that black-out regulations mean what they say. After he'd been warned once or twice, he took off every bulb in his house barring his bedroom. He's got shutters there, and was in the habit of using them, but the shutters have got holes bored in them, and they fit badly. At last his charwoman got the job done, pasted up the holes, and made curtains out of every bit of old rag she could collect from the rest of the house. Anyway, as a black-out it functions all right. You can't see a glimmer at nights now."

"Thanks, that's what I wanted to know," said Reeves. "Incidentally, you don't know where the previous tenants of the studio moved to, do you?"

"No idea. Out of London somewhere. They got the jitters. They just did a bunk one day, but they came back for their furniture a month or two later. D'you want to trace them?"

"Yes. There's one or two points they might help with."

"Hm... m." The Senior Warden pondered. Like everyone else in the neighbourhood he was interested in the Folliner case. "I wondered a bit myself," he said, "though it's best to wonder under one's breath, if you take me. The name of the tenant was Stort—Randall Stort—and a nasty bit of work he was, but a clever painter, I believe. He used to be in and out of number twenty-five, because he had a lady-friend living there for a bit. Old Folliner used to let rooms to anyone who was green enough to take them, and a girl who was supposed to be an artist's model was living on the ground floor there for a month or two before the outbreak of war. I've wondered to myself if Randall Stort had anything to do with Folliner's end. There are such conflicting stories about the old man. Some say he was a pauper, some say a miser."

Reeves nodded. "Yes, and those who believed that he was a miser would have assumed he'd got a hoard put away somewhere. Did you know Stort, personally?"

"Only on account of my job. I've been doing Civil Defence work in this district since '39, and we got to know most of the people in our sections to some extent—first the gas-mask business, then black-out and shelter duties. I spoke to Stort a good many times, and I've been into the studio reading the riot act about his black-out, and giving him advice. He was what I call a mess—and so was his stable mate, a laddy called... what the hell was his name... it sounded French, and I always thought he was a fifth columnist, or worse. Listelle, that was it."

"Did you see any of Stort's paintings?"

"Yes, just to glance at. He did a lot of portraits, bold-faced wenches and shoddy looking men, but they were striking—vigorous work I'd call it."

"Did you ever see a portrait he did of old Folliner?"

The warden shook his head. "No. How do you know he did one?"

"Mrs. Tubbs told us. I suppose you can't remember the name of the firm who moved Stort's furniture?"

"Yes, I can, by gum! I happened to notice—it was Bickford's van. Bright ideas you chaps have."

Reeves laughed. "It'll take a lot of my bright ideas before we arrive at anything. I know the game. We shall trace Stort to some safe little country cottage… and we shall find he didn't stay there for long. Got bored with the fields, or too far from a pub. After a lot of trouble we shall trace him to three or four other places, and then find he came back to London one night and got his ticket in a raid. I'm used to that story."

The warden laughed: "I should never have thought you were a pessimist—you don't look one. Incidentally, it was Stort and Listelle who dug that hole in the garden of 25, silly fools! I had one good laugh over them: I bet the only time they'd ever bent their backs to a spade was when they made their 'dug-out.' They were frightened stiff, both of them. It took fear to make them work."

"How old were they?"

"Stort might have been 50, or a bit less. Difficult to tell. He was grizzled, and face lined a bit. Listelle was younger, but he was an undersized little rat—typical C3. None of the services would have looked at him. Incidentally, you know the studio and garden—so called?"

"Yes."

"Well, you'll have noticed that the gardens of Hollyberry Hill back on to Sedgemoor Avenue. Stort used to frequent a pub called the Spotted Dog; he painted their signboard incidentally. He found out that his quickest way home from the pub to the studio was by the garden of the house in Sedgemoor Avenue which backs on to 25 Hollyberry Hill. He'd got the devil of a cheek: he kept a ladder on his side of the wall, and drove a staple into the brick-work on the other side, and used that to give him a leg-up over the wall. The tenants reported it to the police—the Sedgemoor Avenue tenants that is—but he was never caught, although I know he often used his short cut. I wondered if he'd used it again. He'd have had a latch-key to number 25, and so would Listelle, probably."

"That's jolly interesting," said Reeves, his intelligent eyes very bright.

The warden looked rather worried: Reeves guessed he was a conscientious fellow, not given to careless gossip.

"I don't want to give you a wrong impression," said the warden. "You know how it is with these artist blokes, they seem queer fish to ordinary careful chaps like me, and I may be doing them an injustice. I didn't like Stort, but Listelle was even nastier. I'd back him as the likelier of the two when it came to dirty work."

"Anything solid to go on, or just a hunch?" asked Reeves.

"Just guess-work," replied the other. "Stort was an obstinate, tiresome beggar, but Listelle was cunning—he'd always got an answer to everything, and he was plausible as they make 'em. I've just thought of something which might interest you. Listelle used to play darts up at that pub just off the High Street—the Green Dragon. He was a wonderful darts player I'm told. One of our fellows used to go there, and he said Listelle used to spin yarns about an old miser he

knew—said he used to spend the nights counting up his treasure…
It might be worth your while to go up there and see if you can get
any information."

"Good. I'll follow that up," said Reeves. "Is the chap who told
you about it still at your post?"

"No. He was called up last year. He's in Iceland I believe. Look
here. I'm worried about this," said the warden. "I'm telling you a
lot of hearsay and guess-work, and come to think of it, you may be
thinking I'm a bit too forthcoming with my suggestions. I suppose
a warden, like me, might be said to have opportunities of house-
breaking and all that."

Reeves laughed. "Don't you worry about that! I reckon you
were on duty at the post between eight o'clock and ten last
night."

The warden grinned sheepishly. "Yes. I was. Thanks be for that."

"O.K.," said Reeves. "Now the chap who really interests me of
these two is Stort, because you say he was the one who used to
climb the Sedgemoor Avenue garden. You never heard of Listelle
doing that?"

"No. I don't think so. It was Stort the old lady mentioned, and
I think she knew 'em by sight all right. I'd give a lot to know if he
did come and climb that wall last night. In a way, it'd have been an
easy job to do—and I can't see how you can ever prove anything."

"Well, to start with it's a matter of finding Stort and asking him
just what he was doing last night," said Reeves.

"And if he's faked an alibi?"

"It's not nearly so easy to do as people believe," said Reeves.
"Most people break down under examination when they're lying
because it's very difficult to lie consistently. However, no use counting one's chickens. I've got to find him first."

"Well, if I come across anyone who knows anything about him, I'll let you know," said the warden. "Our chaps do pick up a bit of gossip one way and another. I only hope I'm not setting you out on a wild-goose chase, because I don't know anything against either of these chaps, except that Stort made free with the old lady's garden, and Listelle spread rumours about old Folliner being a miser."

"If nobody ever told us any ideas that came into their heads we should have a poor time in my job," replied Reeves. "It's chaps like you who're willing to help who give me a chance. Any other ideas thankfully received."

"Good! I'll tell you if anything occurs to me," replied the warden. "You see I'm particularly interested in this case of yours, because I've lived around here nearly all my life. My father had a house in Hollyberry Hill—one of those derelict ones at the Dayton Crescent end—and father knew old Folliner when he was a reasonable being. It's true he was very well off at one time. He had a builder's and decorator's business and owned some property as well. I believe he had a reputation as a very hard man—he was down on his poorer tenants I believe, but he was respected. He paid his debts and was straight. It's only of recent years he's got so eccentric. Some people say he speculated and lost all his money, and that turned his head. Other people say he became miserly and hoarded it, but nobody knows for certain. I lived over the other side of Hampstead for some years, and lost sight of him. When I came back here I was amazed to learn he was still alive. He must be over ninety now, about the same age as my own father would have been had he lived. Think of it. 1850 to 1940. What a period to have lived through! Some folks say there's been more change in the world in those hundred years than in the whole thousand years preceding. Progress? My hat! Do you call it progress?"

"Depends where you're progressing to," said Reeves. "Sometime these past two years I've thought human beings were making a bee-line for hell. If your dad passed out before the nineteen-forties, I reckon he was luckier than old Folliner."

"I reckon he was," said the warden fervently.

CHAPTER EIGHT

I

AFTER REEVES HAD LEFT THE AIR RAID WARDEN'S OFFICE, HE returned to number twenty-five, entered by the front gate, and walked round to the back. The path had once been gravelled, but now it was what Reeves described as "a muddy mess." The gravel had long since been washed away or ground into the sooty London soil, and to-day there was another good reason for the decrepit appearance of the "path." The A.F.S. had been called in to pump out the water from the dug-out, and their hose had been dragged through to the back garden. Reeves went on, past the main entrance to the studio, whose door was only six or seven feet away from the ground-floor windows of the house. Reeves, studying the lay-out, thought it probable that the studio had been built in the first place for the use of the owner of number 25, and it seemed likely that a covered way had been arranged from the french window of the house giving access to the studio. The further end of the studio building, where the "K. and B." was situated, was probably a later addition. The small window of the studio gallery, where Rosanne slept, was on a level with the first-floor window of the house.

Reeves walked down the length of the studio and noticed that Bruce Manaton stared at him from a window—stared resentfully, as though he were exasperated by the intrusion into his privacy.

The dug-out was empty of water now: it had been planned as a deep trench, but the unsupported walls had slipped, and it was now a shapeless, malodorous muddy hole, flanked by the pile of clay which had been excavated by the diggers. This had been thrown against the garden wall on the north side, and the wall had partially collapsed as a result.

Reeves walked on, past the back entrance of the studio, until he reached the wall dividing the garden from that of the garden in Sedgemoor Avenue. The wall was about eight feet high, and in very poor condition. Reeves easily found a gap in the brick-work which assisted him to climb up, and a moment later, with the agility of a monkey, he straddled the wall and looked over into the other garden. He found himself facing an irate elderly woman who was armed with a rake, and so baleful was her glance that he wondered if the rake would be used in a frontal attack on himself.

"Young man, this is an outrage," she declared, and her voice was such a deep bass that Reeves was positively startled.

"I think that's putting it a bit strongly, madam," he protested pleasantly. "I'm only doing a bit of reconnaissance work. I say, I do like your garden. I'm a bit of a gardener myself when I'm off duty, and it's a real pleasure to see a place so well-kept."

Reeves generally managed to say the right thing when he wanted to, and his spontaneous sounding (but calculated) appreciation had just the effect it was intended to have. The stalwart lady grounded her rake and looked at Reeves quite amiably. Reeves guessed her age to be about sixty, her status that of an independent spinster, her health excellent, and her character that of "a holy terror."

"I take great pride in my garden," she replied in her booming voice, pushing back her cropped white hair with a muddy hand. "It's wonderful how things grow here. My roses are quite a sight in summer, but the way the neighbourhood is deteriorating is lament-able—lamentable!" she reiterated. "This was once a very desirable and respectable neighbourhood, and look at it now! Crimes abounding at one's very door, privacy disregarded, and everything going to rack and ruin. Bombs I can disregard—we're all in it together—but crime and corruption and disreputability—it's too much."

"Most upsetting for you, madam—and the sight of these derelict houses must be most depressing."

"*Most* depressing. Very depressing indeed," she said. "I had a trellis put up on that wall once, and my polygonum was covering it nicely, but that wretched creature who lived in the studio insisted on its being taken down. He said it interfered with his light—stuff and nonsense! Unhappily that wall is not my wall. I was helpless in the matter."

"Very trying," said Reeves sympathetically. "I have heard that you had a lot of trouble with the studio tenant at one time."

"Trouble! These artists are all alike, no sense of responsibility or decency. I could tell you things you would scarcely credit."

While the formidable lady boomed on, Reeves was examining the further side of the wall. There was no staple in it now to facilitate climbing, but he was quite sure that he would have found no difficulty at all in obtaining a foothold. The path of the further garden was neatly flagged with crazy paving, he noticed, the interstices planted with Arabis and Aubretia and other small plants. So far as he could see there was a trellis gate which shut off the garden from the approach in Sedgemoor Avenue.

"We get to hear some queer stories in my job," he said. "I'm a C.I.D. man, madam."

"I see. Well I suppose detectives have to climb walls and to do other peculiar things," she said, and Reeves bent towards her.

"I hope you haven't been too much bothered with our interrogations, madam. I know it is often very tiresome to be worried with seemingly unnecessary questions."

"No. I have been put to no inconvenience at all—not by the police. An inspector did call, a stout middle-aged man, very civil and respectful, but as I was away last night, I was unable to help him. I was fire-watching, as I habitually do once a week."

"I have an idea that you could give us some help in another way, madam," went on Reeves. "If you could tell me when it would be least inconvenient for you, I should be grateful if you would answer a few questions."

"Any time you like, any time," she responded. "I am seldom out. My name is Miss Stanton, and this house is called 'Ithaca.' A classical name, chosen by my dear father."

"A very beautiful name," said Reeves tactfully. "I will call on you later, madam, and I apologise for my appearance on your wall. We do have to behave like performing monkeys sometimes, all in the prosecution of our duties."

He grinned as he spoke, showing an excellent row of white teeth in his lean angular face, and Miss Stanton boomed out a deep and hearty laugh.

"You appear to be an intelligent and civil monkey," she replied. "I will show you my garden some time. I have Hellebore in flower, and Winter sweet."

"Wonderful, in a London garden, too," said Reeves.

He slipped back to his own side of the wall and brushed his trousers down, indulging in a quiet chuckle which was very full of mirth. "Marvellous old girl," he said to himself. "What the blazes is Hellebore? I must find out."

He made his way back past the studio, where Bruce Manaton stared at him again from the window, and made his way to the front door of number 25.

II

"Inspector Jenkins inside?" Reeves enquired of the constable on duty at the door.

"Yes, he's there, and the Chief Inspector's just come in, too."

Reeves went inside and upstairs to old Mr. Folliner's bedroom. Jenkins, together with a clerk from his department, was still examining the never-ending papers which had been packed into the vast wardrobe. Macdonald was standing by the window.

"I've just been described as a civil and intelligent monkey," said Reeves, "and can you tell me what Hellebore is?"

"Christmas rose," replied Macdonald promptly. "Did she call you that, too? I saw you doing your stuff on the garden wall."

"The things I've done in the name of duty," groaned Reeves. "Anyway, I've been getting a spot of information."

He gave Macdonald a neat précis of his gleanings, and ended up: "What about it? Do I pop round to Bickfords and start in on the good old trail?"

"I think so," replied Macdonald. "You'll probably find that their records were lost in the blitz, their van driver is now a prisoner in the Far East, and no one has ever heard the name of Stort anyway. Now say if both you chaps listen to me for a bit, and give me the benefit of any brain-waves you're likely to have."

Reeves seated himself on the late Mr. Folliner's armchair, Jenkins removed his glasses, and Macdonald leant back against the window and expounded.

"Yesterday evening three people—at least—entered this room. One was Mrs. Tubbs. She left the house just about half-past eight and went in to see Miss Manaton, and left a latch-key on the kitchen table. Mrs. Tubbs did not arrive back at her own home until after

9.15, just as the nine o'clock news was over. She lives in Myrtle Place, about ten minutes' walk in the usual way, but admittedly the fog was very thick. Mr. Verraby, according to his own account, came into the house just after nine o'clock. According to the night watchman, Verraby should have reached this house by five minutes to nine. Neil Folliner says that he got here 'just after nine,' about right according to Private Brown's computation."

Jenkins intervened here. "According to the evidence of the photographs, which shows Neil Folliner's footprints superimposed on Verraby's, Verraby got here first, which fits in with the times."

"Yes. I think we can assume that. Neil Folliner and Verraby both state that the cash-box was lying on the floor, empty, when they arrived. According to Jenkins' researches among deceased's papers, the latter has realised all his property—saving this house—for cash, his transactions being spread over a period of nearly ten years. At the beginning of that period he had a banking account at the City and Westminster, but he withdrew all his money out of deposit in 1938. There is no evidence to show what he did with it."

"He put it in that cash-box," said Jenkins, "I'll lay any money that's what he did with it, and he spent happy hours every evening counting up his notes. I expect he wished it was in gold—misers love gold—but he couldn't get gold, so he had to be contented with notes."

"It's a reasonable assumption," said Macdonald, "anyway for the moment we'll assume that the money was in the cash-box, and that the murderer stole it."

"Half a jiffy," said Reeves. "Was the old chap shot with his own pistol?"

"Yes. There's no question about that. The bullet's been examined and the breech markings prove that it was shot from the pistol found on the floor. This pistol was bought by old Folliner in

1930—the receipt for it is among his papers. The P.M. shows that he was knocked over the head first, and then shot."

Jenkins nodded his solid head. "Yes, and you can make another assumption from that. He recognised the person who came into the room, that's why they shot him. Wanted to make perfectly certain he wouldn't recover and give them away."

"That seems reasonable to me," said Macdonald. "Of course, there are several variations which might be worked out: it's possible that one person shot him, and that another stole his valuables."

"Possible, but I don't believe it," said Jenkins. "The murderer took the loot—I'm certain of it. We've three possibilities at present—one is Mrs. Tubbs, one is Mr. Verraby, and one is Neil Folliner."

"Four," said Reeves. "The fourth is Miss Manaton."

"There aren't any traces of her," said Macdonald. "Of course, Neil Folliner was wearing army boots, heavy things which left imprints on the damp linoleum. Verraby was wearing crepe rubber soles, which also leave a characteristic mark. Mrs. Tubbs was admittedly in the house on her lawful occasions."

"How nearly can they fix the time of death?" asked Reeves, and Macdonald replied,

"That's a point which the medical experts will never swear to—not within minutes. They have been proved wrong too often. The surgeon reached here at 9.40—a very good effort considering the sort of night it was. He said that death had occurred within the hour preceding his visit—possibly more than an hour, possibly less."

"So it's a possibility that Mrs. Tubbs *could* have shot him before she left here?"

"Yes. It's a possibility, among other possibilities."

"She knew—although she denied it—that Neil Folliner was coming: she could have left that postcard handy for you to find."

"Yes. It all fits in quite well, but why did she go into the studio when she left here?"

Jenkins shook his head, rubbing his bristly chin thoughtfully with a wide thumb. "She wouldn't have done it, Chief. You've got to consider human nature as well as possibilities. If Mrs. Tubbs had shot old Folliner and stolen his money, she'd never have gone into the studio and chatted to Miss Manaton like that. Mrs. Tubbs would have gone straight home and hidden the money. Also, it's probable that she'd have denied ever getting to number 25 that evening: she'd have made some story about the fog being too thick, and said she'd got lost. Then there's another point: that chap in the Sappers—Brown—said he heard her singing as she walked towards this house. D'you think she'd have advertised herself as she walked if she'd got in mind to do a job like this? On the grounds of time-table and the mechanics of the thing, I grant you it's a possibility Mrs. Tubbs could have done it. From the point of common sense—and common humanity for that matter—I just don't believe it."

"That's all right, old man—makes sense, and all that, but you can't always measure folk up with common sense and common humanity. You've got to admit human nature does go off the rails sometime. It's worth while bearing in mind that Mrs. Tubbs *could* have done the job, and that Mrs. Tubbs was almighty thick with Miss Manaton. She—Mrs. T.—took a parcel into the studio kitchen when she paid her call there. Herrings. I know, because I saw them. There might have been other herrings, too, but if so, I didn't spot them, and I tell you I put in a bit of work in that kitchen during the night."

"Somehow I think Jenkins is going to be right over this," said Macdonald. "Quite apart from the fact that Mrs. Tubbs seems to be one of the decentest souls God ever made, I think Jenkins scores over his other points. Let's take the next possibility—Verraby. The assumption concerning him is that he got to the house five minutes before Neil Folliner did, shot the old man after first knocking him over the head, and seized the contents of the cash-box. When he heard Neil Folliner shouting downstairs he must have been fairly staggered. Presumably he hid behind the bedroom door, inside the room, and waited for eventualities."

"That sounds improbable to me, Chief," said Jenkins. "Wouldn't Verraby have got *outside* the room, and then waited?"

"One would have thought so, but if he had done so, the light from the bedroom would have reflected on to the wall outside, and down the stairs, and Neil Folliner, being in the dark, would have seen the light. He didn't. He said expressly 'the stairs were dark, but I saw the light under the door.'"

"Let's try again," said Jenkins. "I like to get my assumptions to square with common sense. I can't see Verraby *waiting*, with the light on, like that. He couldn't have known it was Neil Folliner coming upstairs: it might have been anybody. I'd have guessed that Verraby had got outside the bedroom before Neil Folliner got into the hall, and that Verraby hid behind a door somewhere on the landing, and then stepped in and did his stuff."

"All right. That's reasonable enough," said Macdonald. "In either case, Verraby would have had the loot in his pocket. He hadn't a chance of hiding it in this house, or if so, we haven't found it."

"He'd got it in his pocket," said Reeves with conviction. "That's why he left Neil Folliner in the studio and went out to telephone himself instead of sending Manaton or one of the others. Verraby may have got a fair nerve, but not quite enough nerve to risk chatting to the local Super with a great bundle of stolen notes in his pocket. Someone might have asked 'What's that in your pocket, mate?'"

Jenkins chuckled. "Yes, I pass that. I wondered all along why Verraby went and did that telephoning himself. Of course, it'd have been his only chance to hide the loot. Reeves is right in saying Verraby wouldn't have wanted to go into the charge room with the loot in his pocket."

"Very good. Then can either of you suggest where Verraby cached it? Remember he didn't waste any time over getting to the telephone box, or getting back to the studio after he'd 'phoned. In fact he did it as quickly as it could be done. Now in the good old days he could have come prepared with a couple of big envelopes and slipped the stuff into the pillar post—that trick's often been played—but it won't work now. The post-box was cleared at 5.30 p.m., and it wasn't cleared again until 8.30 a.m. next morning, and Mr. Verraby did *not* slip any interesting documents into any post-box he passed last night."

Jenkins cogitated. "Yes, it's a pretty problem... Where the devil *could* he have hidden the stuff on a black foggy night? There aren't hidey-holes ready made in the street. Letter-box of an empty house?"

"I thought of that. I've had Bolter and Willing investigating every empty house he could have passed in the time. No sign of anything, and the ground was soft enough and wet enough to show footprints. Remember, when Verraby got back to the studio, having wasted no time on his errand, he stayed there until the local men turned up, and then he went direct to the station in the van. From the station he went straight home—I know that, too. If he'd hidden the stuff, he'd have had no chance to recover it. It wasn't on him when he was at the station—the Super saw to that. Very civil and efficient, that Super. I thought you'd like to know your psychological guesses on that score were correct."

Jenkins chuckled, but Reeves sat with a frown of concentration on his face, his angular chin resting on his clenched fists.

"Neil Folliner hadn't got the stuff on him, and if he'd thrown it away we'd have found it by now—that's why you had the dug-out pumped dry, wasn't it? Verraby hadn't got the stuff on him. Jenkins says Mrs. Tubbs didn't take it, anyway, it's not in her house. You know, in this story, all paths lead to the studio. They were all in the studio at one time or another. What d'you bet the loot's there, too? Have either of the Manatons been out to-day?"

"Neither of them," replied Macdonald.

"Good. None of the three who left last night took anything away with them. We saw to that. Seems to me it's a case for a fine-tooth comb at the studio."

"No harm in that," said Jenkins. "Very annoying for the tenants, of course, but they'll just have to put up with it."

Reeves was still staring into space.

"A penny?" enquired Macdonald, and the younger man laughed.

"I might ask you the same, Chief. I reckon you've got a few ideas of your own you're hatching out, but I'd rather be left to tumble to them my own way. When you put me on to that idea of the last tenant at the studio—the nasty bit of work named Stort—I sort of felt that you believed the cast wasn't complete in this act—not all the actors present, as it were."

Jenkins chuckled, a deep cheerful sound. "You and your psychic bids," he laughed, "always going a bit ahead of the evidence. You've found traces of three different persons who were in this house some time yesterday evening. Are you looking for traces of a fourth?"

"I've looked all right," replied Macdonald, "but I haven't found any. It's worth while remembering this, though. The traces of footmarks which we've got were made by men with heavy footgear, and the soles of their boots—or shoes—were wet and black, with that adhesive sort of sooty moisture you always get in a London fog. It's quite possible that someone with dry shoes could have walked upstairs and left no sign of their passing."

Jenkins readjusted his glasses. "I reckon the most useful thing I can do is to get on with my secretarial work," he chuckled. "There's fifty years accumulation to be gone through in this cupboard. The top strata are all what I call impersonal documents—records of business transactions. The old chap didn't seem to have had any human contacts for years, but as we work through, I've an idea we shall get to letters which may tell us a bit about him. Cheer up, Reeves! I may have a whole batch of *dramatis personæ* for you to add to your list of invisible entrants. This is the sort of case which suits a man of my weight. Just sit and work the thing out on paper evidence. I'll leave the wall-climbing and that to you—the monkey work, so to speak."

Macdonald put in a question here. "According to your present researches, would you have expected to find a considerable sum of money somewhere on these premises?"

Jenkins nodded. "Yes, Chief. During the past ten years the old chap realised property and investments to the tune of several thousand pounds. He's kept copies of most of his transactions— and I tell you it's no joke trying to decipher his writing and make sense out of it. There's no evidence as to what he did with the money: so far as I can see he didn't invest it, he didn't buy any-thing, and I can't believe he gave it away. His only outgoings were rates and taxes. I shall have to have the Inland Revenue people along some time, he had some lively correspondence with them. I'll try to get some sort of statement out by to-morrow, but so far as I can see at the moment deceased had several thousand pounds—somewhere."

"In his cash-box," murmured Reeves.

III

"I'd like to give this house the once-over again while it's still daylight," said Reeves, as he and Macdonald left Jenkins to his secretarial work.

"Right. We'll go over it together. It'll be an exhilarating experience for you," said Macdonald. "Upstairs to begin with."

Reeves glanced at once at the treads of the stairs before he mounted them: there were footmarks showing in the sooty dust which lay thickly on the bare boards, but these footmarks were all close to the hand-rail side. Macdonald said:

"Yes, the dust has its uses. Those footmarks are ours. No one else has been up these stairs for weeks, probably months. The dust is lying like a pall everywhere, and every footstep shows."

There were four rooms—two front and two back—on the second floor, and a ladder led up to the loft above, in the roof.

"No object in climbing that," said Macdonald. "The loft is bare except for a couple of broken chairs, and some cracked china. I've had the tanks emptied—nothing but soot."

They glanced in at each of the small bedrooms: all four were empty, their walls mildewed and damp-stained, doors and wainscot cracked and peeling. Reeves went to one of the back windows and looked down at the studio roof—sheets of corrugated iron much in need of painting. There had apparently once been a pole for a flag on the gable end of the studio, close to a disused chimney pot.

The pole lay forlornly on the iron roof, and loops of the cord still festooned the gable and hung flapping a yard or two down the wall, tapping miserably in the wind. It was a forlorn and melancholy prospect of an ugly and neglected structure. Beyond Reeves could see into the garden of Sedgemoor Avenue, where Miss Stanton was still busy with her rake.

On the first floor there were also four rooms—two large bed-rooms with small dressing-rooms opening out of them, and in addition was an antique bathroom and lavatory. The only furnished room was Mr. Folliner's bedroom.

"The old man sold everything except the contents of his own bedroom and such junk as even the rag and bone men wouldn't give him a penny for," said Macdonald. "Any broken sticks of furniture or packing cases or anything else which would burn he used for his fire. Not much chance for anyone to hide anything here in a hurry There's the chimneys, and under the floor-boards—we've drawn a blank everywhere."

On the ground floor, in the hall, there was one relic left, a much battered grandfather clock. It had evidently been through a minor earthquake, for its face was broken, its panels cracked, and its door missing. Reeves glanced inside the case: the pendulum had dropped off, the weights and chains were missing.

"Sold the weights and chains and was in process of burning the case," said Reeves. "Any of the works left?"

"Yes, but they're rusted into a solid whole—even the junk man wouldn't fancy them—and old Folliner was no believer in giving things for salvage," said Macdonald. "There's nothing hidden among said works."

They went through the ground floor rooms and cupboards, noted that coal was now dumped in what had once been a cloak room, and that every electric fitting had been cut away from its flex. The big room which had once been the drawing-room of the house, with long windows overlooking the one-time garden, had once been a beautiful room. Now its grimy walls were defaced with smears of paint, smudged over underlying frescoes.

"Hullo," said Reeves. "This is the room Mr. Stort's lady friend must have inhabited. Did he decorate it for her, and if so, what?"

He walked up to the wall and tried to make out the nature of the painting underneath. Macdonald said:

"There were a series of portraits on the wall, apparently, some painted, some in charcoal—and somebody has painted them out. I must ask Mrs. Tubbs if she knows anything about it."

Reeves continued to stare. "Damned funny..." he said slowly. "Did the lady friend get tired of the decoration... or did old Folliner disapprove of it?"

"It's the only room in the house which holds anything of interest," said Macdonald, "but there isn't anywhere to hide anything. Come and see the kitchens, and you'll know what the 'servant-gal' of fifty years ago had to endure."

A staircase with stone treads led down to the dank and dreadful basement. There was a big, dark kitchen, with a stone floor, mouldy and beetle infested. A huge rusty range took up one side, and a dresser the other. The window was heavily barred, and dingy evergreen shrubs pressed their leaves against the cobwebbed glass. The grate of the range was full of burnt fragments, mostly burnt paper. Macdonald chuckled as he saw Reeves look eagerly at the black remains.

"I don't think that any of that is the sort of ash bank-notes would leave," he said. "In any case it's not fresh ash. It's weeks old, at least. I'm getting one of our fellows to come and sort it out and get it analysed. If I try to move any of it, it will disintegrate."

Reeves moved towards the grate, his keen nose twitching a little, and he took out his torch and turned a beam of light on to the ashes.

"What do you make of it?" he asked, and Macdonald replied:

"So far as I can see without touching it it's the remains, amongst other things, of a stout canvas. Perhaps the 'lady friend' used her protector's surplus works of art to heat up the bath water. So far as I can see, this range is the only method of heating the water for the outsize antique upstairs."

"Blimey!" said Reeves. "Well, it's a fair sized Chamber of Horrors this kitchen is."

"Come and see the scullery, it's much worse, and there's a coal cellar and other delights, all with several steps leading down to them—and remember the food and the china had all to be carried up those twisting stone stairs to the dining-room," said Macdonald. "The young servant gal of the early nineteen-hundreds got paid £12 a year for the privilege of working in a house like this."

"And they say the Victorian era was the golden age of prosperity and happiness," said Reeves, as he poked his enquiring nose into the "coal cellar and other delights." "One thing I'll say about the different tenants who dossed down in this abode of bliss, they didn't leave much junk behind them."

"Swept, if not garnished," murmured Macdonald. "One benefit this war has conferred on suffering humanity—it has liquidated the junk of a century. There is hardly any trifle so trifling that it is beneath contempt from a junk merchant's point of view: papers, rags, bottles, bones, boxes… what's the immortal tag—'puffs, powders, patches, Bibles, billets-doux…'"

"How long ago do you reckon it is since this door was opened?" asked Reeves, studying the back door, which boasted two powerful bolts, a heavy chain and an outsize in door-keys.

"Judging from the ivy on the outside, not for two growing seasons at least," said Macdonald. "Whoever came into this house entered by the front door and went out by the same way."

"In other words, possessed a latch-key," said Reeves.

"Not necessarily," replied Macdonald. "They might have been admitted by another party, or found the front door open. Well, having seen the complete exhibition—one period residence, mainly unfurnished—would you like to hazard a guess at the present whereabouts of Mr. Folliner's fortune?"

Reeves turned and studied Macdonald's non-committal countenance.

"I've made my guess," he replied. "Meantime, I'd like to get busy on Mr. Stort. I want to know why his lady friend mucked up those wall paintings."

"All right. Get on with it, and report if you want any help. Where do you think of starting?"

"With the holy terror in Sedgemoor Avenue—the lady with the rake. Christmas rose you said that thing was? Always believe in showing an intelligent interest."

"Very sound, but don't overdo it. Gardeners love answering questions. Good hunting!"

CHAPTER NINE

I

WHEN REEVES HAD LEFT HIM, MACDONALD DID A LITTLE quick thinking regarding his own time-table, and came to the conclusion he had an hour or two to spare which he could devote to the matter of Listelle. Reeves was on the same trail, though Stort was his immediate quarry. Macdonald thought that there might be a chance—admittedly a remote chance—that if Stort and Listelle had come back to the neighbourhood of the studio, the latter might have paid a visit to his old haunt at the Green Dragon. It had happened more than once in Macdonald's experience that a "wanted" man, suspected of having returned to his own neighbourhood, had dropped in for a drink at a familiar pub. The temptation to do so seemed irresistible in certain cases, as though the old habit of "dropping in for another" had overcome caution. Enquiries had already been made at The Spotted Dog, nearer at hand, but without result.

The middle of the afternoon is not a good time for approaching a public-house with the idea of acquiring information, but Macdonald, having made his way to the High Street and found the little alleyway where the Green Dragon was situated, went to the side door of the house and rang the bell. The door was opened by a stout, cheery-faced, grey-haired lady, dressed in a "period" gown of black satin, her vast bosom embellished with gold chains, locket and a huge cameo brooch. Her grey hair was dressed over pads and secured by diamond-studded combs, and her whole appearance was perfect in its consistency. She was a picture of the early nineteen-hundreds, and

Macdonald liked her at sight. Before he could speak, she addressed him reproachfully.

"Nothing doing, dearie. I've told you so before. It's no manner of use you coming worrying me. You've got to take your turn in hours like all the rest."

"Quite right, but I haven't come to worry you about that," said Macdonald cheerfully, and she replied,

"Lor'! You're not the boy I took you for. They're always on to me. Silly, I call it, and it does get my goat when they come worrying at the side door. You'll get me into trouble, I tell 'em—it's an old joke, but none the worse for that. Now what is it you want, dearie?"

"You are the proprietress here?"

"That's right. Me, and my boy Jem helps, ever since my old man went home." She surveyed Macdonald with her shrewd old blue eyes. "If it's not a bottle of Scotch you're after—and you look as though you've too much sense for that—then you're a plain-clothes man. That right? No offence meant."

"And none taken. You're quite right. It's nothing to worry you: I'm making a few enquiries about a man who used to come and play darts here. Can you spare a few minutes for a chat?"

"Come in," she replied at once. "I'm not that keen on having the police in me house, if you follow, but you look a nice fellow. First on the right, and mind the cat."

Through an archway draped with beaded curtains, Macdonald made his way down a narrow passage and into a parlour which made a perfect setting for Mrs. Blossom, the proprietress of the Green Dragon. From the lustres on the chandelier to the shell flowers on the draped overmantel the dim overcrowded little room was unspoilt by a single anachronism. The flowered walls were crowded, with heavily-framed pictures, photographic enlargements, texts, and coloured presentation prints from old journals. In one quick glance round Macdonald saw Wellington meeting Blucher, Cherry Ripe, Bubbles, Shoeing the Bay Mare and the Coronation of Queen Victoria. A family Bible and pile of albums stood on a table shaded by pampas grass, flanked by boxes garnished with shells.

Mrs. Blossom closed the door and seated herself decorously on a shiny horsehair armchair, indicating another to Macdonald.

"Darts?" she enquired. "Is it that Listelle you're after?"

"Quite right," replied Macdonald.

"I said to my Jem, 'I wonder,' I said, and he told me not to wonder too much. 'It's not as though you know anything about him, ma,' he said to me, 'and if he did once live in that there studio, it's not nothing to do with us.' But you can't help wondering, now, can you, 'uman nature being what it is?"

"Of course you can't help wondering," agreed Macdonald, "and my job would be much harder if people weren't interested in their fellow-creatures."

"That's just it, dearie," she agreed. "Life'd be a dull business if we all minded our own business and nothing else. Not that I'm a busybody. I don't gossip—don't hold with it and it ain't good for business—but I *do* take an interest, so to speak. And I got a way of summing people up. I've served in a bar since I was a young girl—and if that's not an education in 'uman nature, I don't know what is."

"You're quite right there," agreed Macdonald. "You must be a shrewd judge of human nature, Mrs. Blossom. What did you make of Mr. Listelle?"

"Too clever by 'alf, and nasty with it," she replied at once. "Talk? He'd keep the saloon bar happy for hours, just the way he talked, and as for stories! My! But I'd pull him up when he got too free: he knew he couldn't take no liberties with me behind the bar. Then 'e played darts a marvel—real skill that was, 'and and eye perfect. Clever with his hands he was, juggling and that. Been on the halls when he was young—he'd still got the patter. Well, there you are. Clever as a monkey, and yet he never had a bean. Talk as large as life, but when it came to the blitz, 'e just crumpled up. Frightened stiff, 'e was, and did a bolt. I can't abide funks, and I told 'im so, straight."

"You saw him again then, after he left London in 1940?"

"Bless you, yes. Always turning up he was. In the summer of '41 he came along one evening. 'So you're still alive, ma?' he asks. 'Small thanks to you I am,' I told 'im, 'and what've you been doing to 'elp beat that 'Itler?' He told me a long rigmarole. Been living in a caravan somewhere near Brighton: then 'e got a job in Eastbourne, and when that got a packet 'e did a bunk to Bournemouth. Then he and his artist friend took a cottage in the country, only he couldn't stand that for long. The fields got him down. He popped in here again last summer; cadged a bed with a fellow he used to know in Grey's Buildings, just at the back there, and sure enough there was a raid again the very first night he came. Not what I call a real raid, not enough to make me get up and put the kettle on, just sirens and a bit of gunfire, but it frightened him silly, all the same. He went off again, and I haven't seem him since. I wondered, though. He used to live in that studio, and I've heard him say the old man next door had thousands... Makes you wonder."

Macdonald nodded. "Quite. Did you ever see the man he shared the studio with—Stort?"

"No. I never saw him. Mr. Listelle he talked about him though. These artists, they're a queer lot. I'll tell you what. Mr. Listelle was a bit of an acrobat. Climb anything, he could. I've seen him doing monkey tricks in my bar. Told him off for it, too. I didn't really fancy him, though he's set me off laughing many a time."

"Have you any idea where he went to when he left London last?"

She shook her head. "No. I never heard no more of him. Bert Brewer might know. Lives in Grey's Buildings: he used to be potman here, but now he's got his pension and a daughter in munitions and he don't work any more."

"Right. I'll go round and see if I can persuade him to have a chat. Have you any idea what Listelle did for a living?"

"I reckon he cadged his way along. He did football pools, backed the dogs—he made quite a bit at that—and once or twice he got commission jobs, selling stuff. He's tried to push some of his stuff over in this bar—always some rubbish. Bless you, there are thousands like him; we get to know them. Never do an honest day's work, just cadge along somehow."

"You haven't heard anybody mention him since you saw him last? I wondered if he'd been seen around here lately."

"If so I haven't heard tell of it, and it's marvellous how news gets round. I'll tell you one thing—if Listelle's anywhere about he'd be seen in a bar somewhere. Couldn't live without a drink. It's a puzzle to me how they find the money for it these days."

A few minutes later Macdonald took his leave, thanking Mrs. Blossom with cheerful courtesy, to which the talkative lady responded,

"You're welcome, and I've enjoyed the chat. Pop in one day when you're passing and have one on the house."

II

Macdonald strolled on slowly in the direction of Grey's Buildings, "just at the back there," as indicated by Mrs. Blossom. He was thinking out a theory of his own, a theory which dovetailed all the evidence as a mental exercise, but which needed a lot of solid fact to give it foundation before it could be justified by being put forward before the authorities. As was often the case during an investigation, Macdonald seemed to happen across "side-shows," which had entertainment value apart from the information he collected. Mrs. Blossom in her parlour was just such a side-show, and the recollection of her would enliven Macdonald's meditations during many a subsequent leisure moment, but in addition to that was the curiously vivid portrait she had given him of Listelle… "Clever as a monkey, and yet he never had a bean. Been on the halls and still got the patter… a bit of an acrobat, climbed anything… just cadged his way along… couldn't live without a drink."

As he walked, Macdonald pondered on his next step. It depended on Bert Brewer. If Bert were a trustworthy fellow, a straight approach might be possible: if Bert seemed a twister, caution would be necessary. Macdonald felt more than ever anxious to meet Mr. Listelle and to discover something of his associates.

Grey's Buildings turned out to be one of those rows of early nineteenth century cottages which still exist in old Hampstead—little two-storey dwellings all in a row, with gardens in front, unseparated by walls. Each cottage had its own paved path, and even in January it was possible to see that the owners took a pride in their gardens. Macdonald knocked on the door of the end cottage and soon found himself looking down at a diminutive old man with a wrinkled face and cheerful blue eyes.

"Mr. Brewer?"

"That's me. If it's gardening you want done, I tell you straight I can't oblige. What wiv me rheumatiz an' me game knee I'm past it. Sorry, but there it is."

"Well, if that's the case, it's no use asking you," replied Macdonald. He guessed at once that though Mr. Brewer did not wish to oblige in the gardening line, he was not likely to be averse from a chat. Chattiness was written all over him. Macdonald leaned against the doorpost and offered a cigarette, which the ancient took cheerfully.

"It's difficult to find anyone who's got time to lend a hand these days," went on Macdonald. "Rheumatism must be a great trial to you—but you manage to keep your own garden in very good order. It's pleasant here."

"Yus. Pleasant it is. Seventy-eight years I've lived here come Easter, though it was a struggle to pay the rent sometimes. My old woman, she was a marvel—worked till she dropped. She was proud of her garden, same's meself."

It took Macdonald a very short time to get on to friendly terms with the old "pot boy," who asked him inside to sit by the fire, evidently aware that the price of a drink was a possibility. The Green Dragon soon entered the conversation, and Macdonald got old Brewer to mention Listelle of his own volition. It appeared that Listelle had more than once put him on to a winner, and Macdonald was too wise to ask how many shillings had gone down the drain on winners who failed to materialise. Eventually, the wily Chief Inspector was able to introduce into the conversation that not only had he himself heard of Listelle but that he was very anxious to get into touch with him. By this time the conversation had rambled on in such a way that old Bert Brewer was quite unaware that he had been led on by his pleasant visitor, and the old man went on garrulously, only too eager to continue,

"'E came and stopped the night, me 'aving said I could give 'im a shakedown and welcome: on that sofa 'e slept, but 'is nerves couldn't stand up to them guns. 'E went in the morning. Now where was it 'e told me 'e was going to?"

That Listelle had told him of his next move, old Brewer was certain.

"Would your daughter know?" asked Macdonald, but Brewer shook his head.

"No. She couldn't abide 'im. Wouldn't sit in the same room wiv 'im. Now where was it? A cottage 'e'd got somewhere, no rent to pay, just got to keep an eye on the 'ouse and do some gardening. Deary me, 'im gardening! 'E don't know an 'oe from a spade. In the country it was, but not that far from a town, and a racecourse. 'E mentioned that speshul. Not by the sea. Couldn't stand the sea."

"Well, that's something to start on," said Macdonald. "Let's go through the places where there are race meetings. Newmarket, Ascot, Epsom, Doncaster, Gatwick, Lewes, Newbury..." He paused here as the old man seemed struck by the name. "That it? Newbury's in Berkshire, a long way from the sea."

"Newbury. Newbury," muttered old Brewer. "That's it, I believe. Newbury. That's it. Just a few miles away, 'e said it was. I tell yer what—'is cottage was in a village the charries used to go through on their way to the races, and there was a big 'ouse nearby where a Duke lived and turned 'is 'ouse into an 'orspital. Stables there was there once. Now 'ow's that? I can't remember the name o' the village, but I reckon I ain't done so bad."

"You've done jolly well," said Macdonald, "and if I find Mr. Listelle shall I give him a message from you?"

Bert Brewer smiled all over his face. "Yus, mister. You can tell 'im 'e owes me five bob. I bet him Golden Gleam—that's a good dog, that is—would win at the Reading Stadium, and so 'e did. I

won seven and six on Golden Gleam, an' if I get that five bob orf
Mr. Listelle I reckon I shall 'ave done a treat."

"Well, say if I produce the five bob and collect it from Mr. Listelle
when I see him," said Macdonald.

Old Brewer was delighted. "Thank you kindly, sir, thank you I'm
sure," he said happily.

Macdonald stood up as though to go, and then added as an
afterthought:

"Did you ever hear Mr. Listelle say if he played chess? I'm fond
of the game myself, and I wondered if I'd ever come across him
over a chess-board."

"Chess? No. Draughts, or dominoes, I've seem 'im play. Not
chess. I remember 'im saying the very thought of chess gave 'im
an 'eadache. 'E'd got a friend—the chap 'e lived with—used to play
chess, go on for hours 'e would, like they do, just staring at the
board. Too slow for our Mr. Listelle. Liked something livelier, 'e did."

"Yes, it's not everybody's game," agreed Macdonald. "What
about the man he lived with, ever see him?"

"No, not so far as I know. An artist, 'e was. Very clever, I believe.
When the blitz started, the two of 'em did a bunk out of London
together: went into the country. Silly, I call it. They wasn't meant
to live in the country, 'adn't any sense that way. The country's all
right for them as is used to it, but if you've lived in a town all your
life, the country just gives you the pip."

"So you wouldn't have expected Mr. Listelle to stay in his cottage
down Newbury way?"

"That I shouldn't, unless it so happened there was a nice pub
'andy—but what's the use of a pub if you 'aven't any money? Beer's
a perishing price these days. Sinful I calls it. Still, there's this to it.
If 'e'd left that cottage and come back to Lunnon, I'd lay my oath

he'd 've come to see me. I'll tell you for why: 'e liked to get a bit of something for nothing, and I told 'im 'e could come an' spend a night here if 'e wanted. 'E makes me laugh, and I reckon it's worth putting up with a bit of inconvenience if I get a good laugh out of it."

Macdonald agreed. Looking round the old-fashioned little room, he said:

"You haven't got a wireless, Mr. Brewer?"

"No, sir. Can't be bothered with 'em. I always goes to sleep when they things is turned on. I'm a bit 'ard of 'earing, and they don't make no sort of sense to me."

"D'you like a newspaper?"

"No, only to see the winners, and Mr. Spragge next door, 'e obliges by telling me. I'm no sort of scholard. Reading's like work to me, and me eyes isn't what they was."

A few minutes later, when Macdonald took his leave, Mr. Brewer was nodding over the fire, muttering "Thank you kindly" at intervals.

III

Macdonald strode back to Hollyberry Hill, putting through a call to headquarters on his way. If Mr. Brewer's memory were to be relied upon and the Newbury district held Listelle and his cottage, there were enough pointers to indicate that cottage to the police in the district. The interviews with Mrs. Blossom and Bert Brewer might turn out to be as a hundred others—wasted time from a detective's point of view, but Macdonald was a patient man. Many a time he had based a case on disconnected fragments put together from seemingly useless conversations. In the present case, he was fitting a theory together from possibilities, and even as he had talked that afternoon his mind had been playing with possibilities. "It takes all sorts to make a world," so ran the old adage, and Macdonald found that the same words could be applied to any of his cases. "All sorts"—men as divers as old Brewer and young Mackellon, Listelle and Robert Cavenish: women as various as Rosanne Manaton, Mrs. Tubbs and Mrs. Blossom. From the chance contacts of seemingly unrelated people, the Chief Inspector built up a theory, and in the process, as someone once said of him, "murdered impossibility, to make what can not be, slight work."

CHAPTER TEN

I

BY TEA TIME ON THE DAY AFTER THE INTERRUPTED STUDIO party, Rosanne Manaton was beginning to show some signs of frayed nerves, unusual in one to whom habitual self-control was second nature. As she lifted down a cup and saucer she caught her hand on the edge of the shelf and the precious cup smashed to fragments on the floor. Rosanne said "Damn" vigorously and unashamedly, and then had to bite her lip to prevent herself crying. "Pull yourself together and don't be an ass," she said. The past eighteen hours had been trying ones. After Macdonald had left the studio the previous night, Bruce Manaton had refused to go to bed. Rosanne had gone up to her gallery bedroom but had been unable to sleep, aware that her brother was prowling restlessly round the studio. He had not put the light out until three o'clock in the morning, and even then Rosanne had lain awake, thinking she heard sounds below. When morning came, Bruce was heavily asleep, and he refused to get up until nearly midday, so that Rosanne was unable to get the studio cleared up. After a late and unsatisfactory meal, Rosanne had suggested that Bruce should go out and give her a chance to get the place cleaned. This he had refused to do, and had wandered about restlessly, getting in Rosanne's way and preventing her settling down to anything.

After a while, Bruce took it into his head to start turning out a chest which contained old tools and working materials—a mess of old paint tubes and brushes and charcoal, wood-engraving tools and blocks, printing inks, block colours and powder colours, and all the

other heterogenous messes collected by a craftsman. Bruce Manaton
was as untidy in his habits as any man could well be; he seemed to
make confusion instantly. If he began looking for materials, or books,
or clothes or papers, the result was always the same—a chaotic
muddle. Rosanne was a tidy and fastidious creature, and she was for
ever working to restore order among her brother's possessions—a
thankless task.

Seeing him rummage in the old wooden chest, Rosanne called
across the studio to him,

"Is it anything I can find for you, Bruce? That lot's mainly junk,
it ought to go for salvage."

"Salvage be damned, I won't have any of my materials chucked
away. It's difficult enough to get stuff. Hell... what's that?"

"That" was a box of powder red, one of the harsh vivid magen-
tas derived from anilines by the modern chemist; the bottom came
out of the box and a cascade of the powder poured down over the
confusion in the chest, over Bruce Manaton's flannel bags, over his
hands, over the floor. "Hell!" he muttered again.

"Oh, for heaven's sake leave it alone and let me clear it up," cried
Rosanne. "It'll be all over everything if you're not careful, and it
stains. It's a filthy colour."

"It's a damned good colour—got some kick in it," retorted Bruce,
and Rosanne laughed.

"Your slacks will show evidence of the 'kick' for the rest of
their natural existence," she said. "I hope you'll enjoy going out in
them. Go out and shake yourself in the garden and see if you can
get it off. It won't wash out, you know—and leave all this to me.
I'll sweep it up. Once we get any water near it, we're done; there's
enough powder there to stain the whole floor. Some colours I can
tolerate, but not that one."

Bruce went outside, leaving a trail of the penetrating powder as he moved, and Rosanne got a broom and endeavoured to clear up the hated colour. She shut the chest and locked it, determined to deal with its contents herself at some later date. When her brother came in again, she said,

"Why not go on with the Cardinal portrait? You can get the lay figure rigged up, Delaunier left his costume for you. You haven't got too much time if you want to get it in for the February show."

"Blast the Cardinal's portrait... I tell you I'm fed up with the bloody thing. It's no good, it never will be any good. It's not a picture, it's just a rotten bit of illustration. I loathe the thought of it."

Rosanne did not answer immediately. She finished her sweeping and took the dust pan and emptied it in the stove, and then walked across to the easel and swung it round so that the light caught the charcoal drawing.

"You're wrong," she said quietly. "It's a good piece of work—one of the best drawings I've seen you do. If it were a dud, I should know. It isn't. It's got strength in it, and the planes are well done. If you don't stick to it, you'll be a fool, and rather a feeble fool."

She left the canvas and went to her own table and found a cigarette and lighted it, and then sat down on the edge of the table. At that moment Reeves passed outside, and Bruce Manaton muttered: "Those blasted police again... they're haunting the place."

"Oh, never mind the police!" cried Rosanne scornfully. "What do they matter to us? Whatever happened—out there—was nothing to do with us, was it? Weren't you in here, drawing Delaunier, when the old man was murdered?"

Bruce Manaton whipped round on her: "If you'd said *you* were in here, too, Rosanne, there'd be nothing to bother about. Oh, hell! You've got a good opinion of me, haven't you? You think that

provided I know *I* am safe, I don't care a damn about you, or anything else."

Rosanne sat very still, watching him.

"You don't think I did it, by any chance, Bruce?"

He came over to her, and put his hands on her shoulders.

"No, my dear. I'm not such a bloody fool as that. I may be a rotter,
Rosanne, and a waster… I may let you work for me, and worry for
me… but I know. Oh, my dear, I know. Do you think I've enjoyed
watching you work like a charwoman, and go without everything
you've wanted, just to keep me out of the gutter—where I belong?
You're worth something. I'm not. If it weren't for me, you'd have
made something of your life."

Rosanne slipped away from the table and from his gripping
fingers, aware that she was trembling. She tried to answer lightly.

"Bruce, I think there's something morbid in the atmosphere of
this place. What on earth has made us all go goopy and get on each
other's nerves? Police at the window?" She laughed a little shakily
and added: "We don't need to indulge in protestations, you and I. We
understand one another well enough without all that. I don't care
a damn about police at the window, Bruce. What I'm afraid of is
having the brokers in, as we did before… Can't you get on with that
portrait? I believe it'd sell, it's going to be a great shouting gorgeous
piece of scarlet, like Van Gogh's Zouave. There's something in the
drawing that's arresting, already. It's much finer than a portrait of
Delaunier. Oh, do get on with it."

Bruce Manaton fumbled on the table, and took Rosanne's last
cigarette.

"All right, Rosa. I'll get on with it. God, when this damned war's
over, let's leave this blighted country and go to Italy again, into the
sunlight. How I loathe this filthy fog, mud and soot and drab dirt."

"Look at your hands, Bruce—dirt but not drabness, stain but not soot. My dear, I told you that red powder would stain."

Bruce Manaton glanced at his hands: they were clammy with sweat, and the red powder paint had turned the palms a livid cerise.

"'It would the multitudinous seas incarnadine,'" he quoted, and again Rosanne laughed.

"'Go, wash this filthy witness from your hands,'" she quoted in return, "or, if you prefer it, 'let each man render me his bloody hand: first yours, Catullus: now Caius Casca, yours...'"

"Oh, for God's sake," cried Manaton, and Rosanne said quickly,

"Oh, don't be an ass. You generally like out-quoting me. I'm going to make some tea. You can't have any sugar, because you've had it all. I shall have to go out and do some shopping, but we'll have tea first."

She went into the "K. and B.," put the kettle on, and was collecting the tea things when she dropped her cup. A moment later Bruce Manaton looked in on her. "What have you done?" he demanded.

"Smashed the nicest cup I possess. We've only got three left now, and one has no handle. What a life! Bruce, go and get on with your work and leave me alone."

He went out and closed the door, and Rosanne waited for the kettle to boil. While she was doing so, she took down a tin box from a shelf and opened it. It was an old-fashioned "spice box," containing smaller boxes to hold cloves and ginger, cinnamon and mace, bay leaves and pepper corns. Rosanne used it now as a cash-box, wherein she kept her money. Bruce had not discovered it yet. She knew, by bitter experience, that if her brother knew where she kept her money he would "borrow it"—as he had borrowed her last cigarette. There were five pound notes in the clove tin, one ten shilling note in the mace tin, and five shillings and sixpence in the cinnamon tin. She took out two pound notes slipped them in her pocket, and replaced the tin.

Just as the kettle boiled, Rosanne heard voices in the studio, and stood with her head cocked sideways, listening. Then the door banged, and there was silence. With the tea tray in her hands, Rosanne went into the studio.

"Wasn't that Delaunier's voice?" she enquired of her brother.

He nodded. "Yes. He wanted to come and pose, but I didn't want him. The sight of him gives me the *cafard* somehow. He's so damned pleased with himself."

"You are an ass, aren't you?" replied Rosanne. "The light's quite good for another hour, and you're all ready to begin painting, and your model turns up—and then you say the sight of him gives you the *cafard*."

"Well, so it does. Never mind, Rosanne, I'll get on with the background. I've got an idea about that, heavy shadow, with a cross light in the corner. I noticed an interesting effect when you had the kitchen door open last night."

"Oh, did you?—and you cursed me to high heaven for opening that door. *This*, my dear, is China tea, and the last Romilly biscuit the world contains, so make the best of it."

"Madonna! How have you got China tea?"

"Saved it. Betty Mountjoy gave me some months ago—honest to God Lap San Suchong. I've been treasuring it like fine gold against an emergency, and somehow to-day I felt justified in using some of it. Everything looked mouldy, and I thought a decent cup of tea might cheer us both up. A pity Robert Cavenish isn't here, he appreciates China tea."

"Cavenish?" Bruce Manaton's dark face grew brooding again. "You like him, don't you, Rosa?"

"Yes. I like him. He's sensible and reliable and kind, and he's not condescending, nor yet a complete Philistine. Do you know, he writes good verse, Bruce. Don't tell him I told you, but Cavenish is a poet manqué. Rather pathetic. He works all day on Government reports at the Home Office, and he's capable of writing poetry which compares well with T. S. Eliot's."

"Cavenish? Good God! I know he can play chess—but *poetry!* I suppose you're the only person in the world who knows about it. Why don't you marry him, Rosanne?"

"A. He hasn't asked me to. B. I don't want to and shouldn't if he did. I'm not of the marrying variety. If I'd wanted to get married, I could have done so. Have some more tea."

Bruce pushed over his cup.

"All my fault," he said morosely.

"You flatter yourself," retorted Rosanne. "I have a mind of my own. Heavens! What's that? Delaunier come back again? If it is, I'm going to tell him to pose for you, and you can get on with it, *cafard* or no *cafard*."

II

It was not Delaunier. When Rosanne opened the studio door she saw Macdonald standing there. Quaintly enough, the first thought which flashed into her mind was, "How clean he looks." Macdonald, tall, neat, in a well-cut dark suit, immaculate collar and black tie, made a striking contrast to Bruce Manaton, who had omitted to shave that morning.

"You are the Chief Inspector, aren't you? Do you want to see my brother? Come in."

Rosanne stood back from the door, and Macdonald saw the studio in daylight, with its dingy shabbiness unsoftened by the play of shaded lights. Bruce Manaton stared at the C.I.D. man with his customary hostile look, and Macdonald said:

"Good-afternoon. I'm sorry to have to bother you again."

"Needs must," said Rosanne: she smiled as she spoke, and Macdonald smiled in return.

"When the devil drives," he capped her remark, adding, "the devil drives us all alike, me, and you, and the world in general these days."

"That's true," said Rosanne. "Do you like China tea? There's still some in the pot."

"I do. I like it very much indeed," said Macdonald, "but it's not fair to drink other people's China tea these days."

"Well, it's here, so if you'd like it you can have it. The other cup hasn't got a handle, but that's not uncommon these days. Do sit down."

Rosanne sounded calm and cheerful and sensible, talking as she crossed the studio to fetch the cup from the kitchen. Bruce, sitting hunched up in his chair, enquired abruptly,

"That young chap—Neil Folliner—do you think he did the shooting?"

"I don't know yet," replied Macdonald. "We're still considering all the possibilities."

Rosanne returned, and poured out a cup of tea and handed it to Macdonald, saying,

"What do you think of my brother's study of the Cardinal?"

Macdonald held out his cigarette case to her, and Rosanne took a cigarette saying,

"Thanks. Bruce just smoked my last one."

Cup in hand, Macdonald went and stood in front of the canvas and studied it, while he sipped his tea appreciatively. At length he said,

"It's impossible for a non-expert to assess the skill of work like this. I think it's a grand drawing. It seems to me that it's not only a striking portrait, it's an impressive composition, too. Even in outline it's got depth—mass—something more than mere line."

"You mean it's three-dimensional," said Rosanne. "You've made a most intelligent commentary. Imagine it with the scarlet and cerise, and Delaunier's black-browed face. Wouldn't you like to buy it when it's finished?"

"Really, Rosanne!" protested her brother. "The Chief Inspector hasn't come here to buy a picture."

"Nor yet to drink China tea," replied Macdonald, "but having accepted the tea, I see no reason why he shouldn't enjoy the picture. You didn't do all that in one sitting, did you?" he asked of Manaton.

"No. Two. I blocked the main proportions in on Tuesday, and the details—face and hands—last night. Damn all! It might have been my best picture, if only... Oh, well. What have you come to tell us?"

"I'm afraid I've come to make a nuisance of myself. We believe it probable that old Mr. Folliner was robbed. We don't know yet who the murderer was, nor the thief, but we do know that three people who were in that house last night also came into this studio."

"Which three?" demanded Rosanne.

"You know that already. Young Folliner, the Special Constable, and Mrs. Tubbs. We have searched the house, and found nothing. We have searched the garden and drained the dug-out, as you know, and found nothing."

"And now you want to search the studio," said Rosanne. "Well, search away. I have no objections to offer. If you find any beetles—and you will—please kill them."

Macdonald's lips twitched, and Bruce put in:

"I don't think my sister was referring to 'beetle crushers,' Chief Inspector. She's much too polite."

"I'm sure she is," replied Macdonald, "but I will deal faithfully with the beetles if I find any."

Bruce Manaton went on: "I can't quite see your point about searching here, all the same. Neither young Folliner nor the Special had the faintest chance of hiding anything while they were here. We were all watching them—five of us—and the thing is just impossible. As for Mrs. Tubbs—well, we just don't believe it."

"There's nothing like looking facts in the face, Bruce," Rosanne's voice was calm and clear. "I was out in the black-out last night, and that latch-key was on the kitchen table. So far as I am concerned, I say 'search,'—as thoroughly as possible." She turned and looked at Macdonald. "I wonder... if I were the guilty party, should I have had the nerve to leave that key on the table, just to look innocent?"

"I don't know," said Macdonald. "I deal mainly in facts, you see. It is a fact that you had not handled the key since Mrs. Tubbs grasped it. The prints on it were fragmentary, but very clear. They were not your prints. I'm not an expert at fingerprint reading, but the difference between the lines on your hands and fingers and those of Mrs. Tubbs are very marked."

"Well I'm damned!" There was marked relief in Bruce Manaton's voice. "And I wanted to chuck that blasted latch-key into the dug-out," he went on, "only Rosanne wouldn't let me. Look here, do you want us to clear out while you search the place?"

"Certainly not. We'll be as little nuisance as possible. I've got a very skilled helper—a woman—and we'll leave everything exactly as it was."

"You're going to have some fun when you hunt through my brother's painting materials," said Rosanne. "You probably have no idea what dirt and mess and muddle mean. Now you're going to find out. You won't look quite so clean when you have finished."

"I expect that I know as much about dirt and mess and muddle as anybody in this world, and a lot more about it than you do, Miss Manaton," replied Macdonald. "A detective's work leads him into strange places, most of which are neither clean nor tidy nor pleasant. I have been in studios beside which this one looks like the abode of an academician. As for kitchens—have you seen the one in number 25?"

"No, thank heaven. I haven't, the old man's room was quite enough. I've got to go out, Chief Inspector, or we shan't have anything to eat for supper. I'll leave you to ransack the place. I don't care what you look at, though it would be all the same if I did. I know that."

"It's true that a woman detective will look through your personal belongings, Miss Manaton, since you have given permission. I know it's repugnant to have one's belongings searched, but it's a very impersonal search."

"Thanks. I understand what you mean. I doubt if any woman in the world has fewer personal belongings than I have—you can look through them yourself for all I care." She nodded towards the gallery. "Now I'm going to do some shopping, and I'll leave you to it." She turned to Bruce. "You might as well get on with that painting. It's suddenly occurred to me, it may be valuable, apart from its artistic possibilities."

She broke off, nodded to Macdonald, and went out by the kitchen door. A moment later Macdonald saw her pass the window, fastening up her coat collar as she walked.

III

Bruce Manaton stood before his canvas with brooding eyes, a deep frown of concentration on his face. Macdonald stood in the centre of the studio, his hands in his pockets, considering the general lay-out. The long barn-like structure ran east and west, the west end nearest to the house. The corrugated iron of the pent roof was covered with some material like asbestos, now stained and discoloured. The north light was set in the sloping roof towards the eastern end. At the west end was the small gallery, with a ladder leading up to it: a curtain—or rather several curtains of varying material—screened the gallery from the floor; otherwise it had only a hand-rail supported by occasional bars. The kitchen door was at the farther end, in the southeast corner of the studio. The stove, an old-fashioned iron affair, stood so that its iron chimney-pipe ran up to the roof just clear of the gallery. There was a blocked-up fireplace in the west wall, under the gallery, and Macdonald guessed from the general arrangement that the gallery had been added some time after the original structure was put up, and that the iron stove superseded the original fireplace. The space under the gallery held a divan bed and a chest of drawers, as well as a number of boxes, old easels, canvases, drawing boards, a small printing press, portfolios, and piles of books, mostly stacked on the floor against the wall. The "front door" of the studio was in the north-west corner under the gallery, with a screen and a curtain arranged for necessities of black-out.

Macdonald took in the whole arrangement very quickly, checking up on the impression he had gained the previous evening, when the different lighting had made the place seem larger and more mysterious. Now, in the cold grey light of late afternoon, the studio looked shabby and sordid.

"What did she mean?"

Bruce Manaton was still standing inspecting his canvas, and Macdonald turned at the question, guessing that it referred to Rosanne's parting remark.

"I expect your sister meant that your picture will acquire a 'sensation value,' so to speak," said Macdonald. "It's not often that artist and sitter are likely to be called as witnesses in a murder case. If it weren't for the war, you'd have had a crowd of cameramen here demanding facilities for photographing your canvas, yourself, and your sitter."

Manaton frowned more deeply than ever, and turned away from the canvas.

"That settles it," he said. "I loathed the sight of the damned thing before, now it nauseates me. Oh, hell, who's that?"

"My department," replied Macdonald. "I need an electrician to fix an adequate light. I'll explain in a minute."

He went to the door and admitted a man and a woman, while Bruce Manaton stood and stared. The woman—a neat, sensible-looking creature in a well-cut suit and natty hat, went straight up the steps to the gallery at a word from Macdonald, and the man betook himself to the kitchen end.

"He wants to look at your fuse-boxes and so forth," said Macdonald. "We don't want to blow all your fuses. It's like this: in a case of this kind we don't want to waste time—or to irritate you—by a detailed search of everything. Given a proper light, it's possible to tell if things have been moved recently—dust deposits tell us a lot. We shan't bother about the books and boxes and so forth which obviously haven't been moved or opened for weeks. An expert searcher can tell that at a glance."

Manaton nodded. "I see. You've got an idea that some body

came in here and just shoved something among the junk. Well, I suppose it's not impossible. It's extraordinary how little one notices of another person's actions if one's not concentrating on them."

"It is. Ask any conjurer. He depends for his success on the fact that few people can concentrate on more than one point at one time. While I'm waiting for the electrician to get a flex fixed up, will you tell me anything you happen to know about the previous tenant in this place?"

"I don't know anything about them, except that they were dirty tykes. Ask Rosanne. All the sink runaways were stopped up, and there was the filth of ages everywhere."

"Did they leave anything interesting—paintings, or anything of that kind?"

Bruce Manaton snorted. "If they'd left any canvases I might have been grateful to them. Have you any idea how difficult it is to get a thing like this?" He indicated the canvas on his easel. "Why are you interested in the last tenants?" he added.

"Because it occurs to me that the last tenants might have been interested in their eccentric landlord. There were some paintings on the walls of one of the downstairs rooms in number 25 which interested me. Portraits, I think. They have been obliterated, painted out with rough smudges."

Manaton stood and pondered, his face frowning. "I don't know anything about them," he said. "I didn't paint them, if that's what you're getting at."

"No, that hadn't occurred to me. From what's left of them I should say they're miles below your standard. I just wondered if the previous tenant had left a self-portrait anywhere about. If one of the frescoes in that house represented Mr. Stort—well, it's been very carefully obliterated, that's all. Do you mind if we black-out now, then we can get going."

IV

While Macdonald searched, Bruce Manaton prowled restlessly round the studio, watching.

The electrician had fixed up his flex, and he carried round a portable lamp whose harsh brilliance threw a vivid white light into every corner. Its merciless beam showed up dust and cobweb, smudge and stain, and Manaton began to understand what Macdonald had said about being able to tell if things had been moved recently. If the light beam was penetrating and thorough, so was the work of the two searchers. Swift, dexterous and amazingly quiet, the Chief Inspector and his helper "inspected" with a thoroughness which left nothing to chance. Bruce Manaton pulled out a drawing-board and began to block in a composition with a carpenter's pencil.

"Detectives at play," he said to Macdonald. "You get some damned queer light effects with that outfit of yours. My God! Imagine that I *had* hidden something in this place, and had to stand helpless and watch while you searched, watching you get nearer and nearer. I should go raving mad, stark staring mad... That fireplace was blocked years ago, incidentally. It was a damned idiotic place to put a fireplace anyway."

The fireplace was very effectively blocked, with a sheet of metal nailed up to the surround. Having inspected it, Macdonald came out into the main part of the studio and glanced at Manaton's sketches.

"Lord! I wish I could draw like that—it's uncanny how you do it, a sort of major miracle."

The sketches represented Macdonald and his assistant peering into a corner, their figures in black silhouette while the white glare of the portable lamp was somehow conveyed by contrast with the black cast shadows.

"Well, I've had some varying experiences in the course of my detective career," said Macdonald, "but I've never been made a picture of while on duty."

"And I've done some queer things during the course of my painting career," replied Manaton, "but I've never been in my own studio and watched the police ransack my belongings. Be careful with that box: there's a lot of very virulent red powder-paint upset inside it—and it's tenacious. I don't believe it ever comes off."

Macdonald and his man made "a good job" of the studio. Apart from the confusion of Bruce Manaton's materials, the place was very sparsely equipped. Two beds to sleep on—and not overmuch bedding—a couple of tables, half a dozen chairs, a minimum of china and glass and kitchen equipment: the place was furnished with bare necessities and no more. The woman detective who had been sent up to the gallery bedroom to search Rosanne's quarters spent but a short time in her task. She said to Macdonald afterwards:

"She's got as many belongings as would fill a good-sized week-end case. No books, or letters, no pictures, or pretties, no cosmetics or creature-comforts."

When Macdonald had finished, Bruce Manaton said to him:

"Well, did you find anything interesting?"

"From a detective's point of view, nothing," said Macdonald.

The painter grinned, not unmaliciously, Macdonald thought.

"The answer's a lemon, then. Can't say I enjoyed seeing you at it, but I'm glad it's over and done with. I'm glad my sister kept out of the way while you were on the job. I haven't much pride left. It's a luxury which the penniless are better without, but Rosanne still retains a few Bourgeois complexes." He paused, and then added: "I'd like to tell you something else, just because you're the sort of chap you are. Yesterday evening, after that poor devil of a Tommy had been haled off in your Black Maria, we talked things over. Rosanne said she had been outside in the black-out. I wanted her to say she'd been in here, with us, all the time. We'd have sworn to it, you know—even Cavenish, with his nice sense of ethics. She wouldn't have it. She preferred to tell the truth." He leant forward towards Macdonald with his dark eyes blazing in their deep sockets. "If you think that Rosanne had anything to do with murder, or theft—well, God help you for the bloodiest fool who ever aped intelligence."

Macdonald stood perfectly still, his grey eyes meeting the other's furious regard.

"I might hazard another question, though I don't expect you to answer it," he said. "Why were you so anxious that it should be established that your sister was not out in the black-out just before nine yesterday evening?"

He did not wait for Manaton to answer, but turned towards the door, adding, "In my job a lot of things have to be done which can be regarded as repugnant in the ordinary way of life. Only one thing justifies them, the fact that crime—crimes of meanness and envy and malice and violence—are the most repugnant of all. Meantime, I'm grateful to you and to your sister, for making it possible to do a necessary job here without protest on your parts. I realise all that that implies."

Manaton drew a deep breath, and flung something across the floor. It was the fragments of a pencil which he had snapped between his fingers.

"I hope to God you've finished," he said.

CHAPTER ELEVEN

I

ROBERT CAVENISH HAD LIVED IN THE SAME HOUSE FOR YEARS, a small house off St. John's Wood High Street, which was run for him by a competent married couple—a Mr. and Mrs. Elliott, an elderly pair who regarded the house as their own home, and whose pride it was to make Cavenish comfortable.

On the evening after the party in the Manatons' studio, Ian Mackellon came in to see Cavenish about eight-thirty. The younger man produced a pocket chess set, saying,

"I've set out the pieces as we left them last night."

Cavenish made a wry face. "You would. Trust a Scot to remember the details of a game. Somehow I don't fancy continuing that particular game. It was yours anyway."

Mackellon laid down the wallet which held the miniature pieces. "You know, I've the oddest feeling that yesterday evening's proceedings formed a sort of pattern—a game of chess with living players."

Cavenish moved uncomfortably in his chair. "Maybe, but I can't regard human beings as pieces on a board. The more I think the thing over the more uncomfortable I feel about it."

"Why?" Mackellon shot out his abrupt question, and then studied the other with observant eyes. He continued at length:

"From seven forty-five until nine o'clock yesterday evening, you and I faced one another over a chess-board: during that same period Manaton and Delaunier faced one another across a model's platform." He paused, and then added, "I wish that Rosanne had been in the studio all the time, too, but I think you were right in insisting that the facts had to be stated, and not tampered with."

"Yes. I don't regret insisting on that: what fills me with discomfort was the way in which Manaton *wanted* to tamper with the facts, as though…"

He broke off, and Mackellon finished his sentence for him, "as though he believed that Rosanne knew something about it."

"That's it—a loathsome suggestion. I wish to God I could get Rosanne right away, out of that shoddiness which invests her brother and his affairs. I can't stand that man Delaunier."

"Here, steady on! It was through Delaunier you got to know the Manatons. Delaunier is a first-class chess player, though he's not a first-class actor. It never occurred to you to dislike him until you saw him in contact with Rosanne Manaton. Incidentally, I shall be surprised if Delaunier doesn't come in here some time this evening. I saw him at lunch; he rolled into my pub and held forth: he's fancying himself in the role of detective."

Cavenish frowned. "He'd fancy himself in any role, confound him. What's it got to do with him, anyway?"

"No more than it's got to do with any of the rest of us, but inevitably one is interested. I don't pretend that I'm lofty-minded enough to banish the whole thing from my memory and pretend I'm not interested. For one thing, I shall never be able to forget the moment when that blustering ass of a Special butted in on us, dragging that tallow-faced laddie by the arm. It was the sort of thing which stuck in one's mind. You know, every one of us was convinced that young Folliner hadn't anything to do with it. Just sentiment, I suppose, because he was hurt, and looked green, and was in khaki."

"Mr. Delaunier, sir." Mrs. Elliott held the door open and Delaunier followed her into the room.

"'Evening, both of you. Hullo, finishing your game at long last?"
Delaunier seemed to take the room in at a glance, and his eyes studied the little chess pieces. "Black to move, and mate in four moves,"
he said, "but black hasn't moved yet. The pieces are as they were
when you left the game last night."

Cavenish nodded, and closed the wallet. "Yes. I don't feel like
going on. I've given Mackellon the game."

Delaunier laughed. "Throwing your hand in? That's a mistake.
I could pull that game out of the fire for you and force a stalemate,
at least."

Mackellon smiled, his hazel eyes glinting. "You've got a damned
good memory, Delaunier."

"Yes, so far as chess is concerned, I've a very good memory.
Well, I've been prowling around the scene of the crime, and a few
interesting points have emerged. I'm more than ever disposed to
credit that pompous Special Constable with the onus of the affair."

Cavenish said nothing, beyond indicating a chair by the fire, and
Mackellon, sitting on the edge of the table, began to fill his pipe,
asking, "Why?" in that terse abrupt manner of his.

Delaunier settled himself comfortably in the chair and lighted
a cigarette.

"The name of the 'Special Gentleman' is Verraby—Mr. Lewis
Verraby. He's fairly well known in the district, it appears. He has
the pleasant habit of buying up building land as cheaply as possible and making a fortune out of it by building flats and letting
them as dearly as possible. That block on Vernon Hill is one of
his major crimes—a blot on the landscape, and twelve foot by
twenty for each tenant at a rental of £120 a year, heating and
C.H.W. provided."

"Interesting, but I don't see that it's relevant," said Cavenish.

Delaunier laughed. "Then you'll never make a detective. Everything concerning any contact in a case is relevant." He broke off, and then asked, "Did either of you fellows notice if the Special or the Tommy was wearing gloves yesterday evening?"

Cavenish shook his head, but Mackellon replied immediately, "The Special was wearing gloves—pigskin ditto, with buttons, fleece-lined, probably costing a couple of guineas the pair. Young Folliner had been wearing a pair of mitts, presumably: he'd got the left one on, the right was missing."

"Very good, very good," said Delaunier. "To get back to Cavenish's 'irrelevancy.' Some months ago, Mr. Verraby purchased a couple of houses in Hollyberry Hill, the ones adjacent to Folliner's. It seemed a senseless sort of purchase—two old houses, hardly fit for reconditioning, until you consider Verraby's habits. If he has bought *two* houses in that block, it's quite probable that he is the owner of the remainder which are unoccupied. He is not, however, the owner of number 25—though it's pretty certain he wanted to be."

Mackellon was studying Delaunier with smiling concentration. "I see your drift, but it's a far-fetched motive. Incidentally, where did you grub all this up?"

"The local, my dear chap, the local. Always try the nearest house of refreshment. The Hollyberry Tavern was seething with excitement. Incidentally, they've still got some dry Martini—a rarity, these days. Now I ask you, assuming that Mr. Lewis Verraby is the owner of those very unpleasant relics of Victorianism which constitute numbers 23 to 29 Hollyberry Hill inclusive, don't you think it's probable, to put it mildly, that he has at some time or other approached the owner of number 25 with a view to purchasing that undesirable property?"

Mackellon nodded, his eyes very alert. "Yes, if you're right in your previous surmise about the purchase of adjoining property, I agree."

Cavenish spoke here. "Very ingenious, but I doubt if any jury would convict on such a motive."

"I wonder," said Delaunier softly. "Put together all that we know of deceased—"

"—which amounts to almost nothing in my case," said Cavenish dryly. "I know that he is the Manatons' landlord, that is all."

Delaunier turned to Mackellon: "Can you add anything to that?"

"Only what the Manatons have told me—that Folliner was a miserly old skinflint, and that his domestic habits were of an unsavoury nature."

"Yes, that he was a miserly old skinflint," repeated Delaunier. "Do you think that such a man would accept a reasonable offer for his property? He probably knew that his land was an island site situated in the centre of a block already sold. He would have held out for his own price. A very irritating matter for a speculator in land-values... A miser... Isn't that the point?"

"Perhaps, but I doubt very much if your theory would stand," said Cavenish. "Also, it's as well to remember that there is a law of slander."

"Oh, that!" Delaunier snorted contemptuously, and then went on: "I'm interested in the 'contacts,' so to speak. Take all those persons, apart from the police, who were in the Manatons' quarters at one time or another yesterday evening. Name them!" he demanded of Mackellon and the latter complied.

"The three of us present here, plus Manaton and his sister, Mrs. Tubbs, Neil Folliner, and Mr. Verraby—unless you include the latter with the police."

"Oh, no, not for the purposes of this argument. Now how many of those persons has had first-hand contact with deceased? The Manatons, in the relation of tenants to landlord; Mrs. Tubbs, who worked for old Folliner—for charity rather than profit, I gather; Neil Folliner, relative of deceased; Mr. Lewis Verraby, probably a business associate."

"Go on," said Mackellon, and Delaunier looked up quickly.

"Haven't I covered the ground, or have *you* any association with the dead man?"

"No, I haven't, nor Cavenish, I believe—but haven't you happened across him? Didn't you say that you'd been to the studio when some previous tenants had it, and that you'd seen old Folliner then?"

Delaunier grinned. "You've a damned good memory, Mackellon, as you said to me a while ago. Yes. I did know the previous tenants a little—in actual fact, I told Bruce about the studio, when he was worrying around hunting for a place to paint in. This one had the merit that all the glass was intact—rather a rarity these days. I probably warned him that the owner was a nasty old customer, too, and that no decorations would be done. That's as far as I can go. To the best of my knowledge I haven't set eyes on old Folliner. Rather a pity: the number of contacts all add to the complexity of the design."

Robert Cavenish made an impatient movement. "I've no patience with that sort of jargon, Delaunier. There's nothing amusing about murder, and being at close quarters to a case, as we happened to be in this one, doesn't excuse being flippant about it."

Delaunier's dark eyebrows shot up. "You can only take pleasure in fictitious corpses, *mon cher*," he replied, his lively dark eyes glancing towards Cavenish's bookcase, "or do you read Michael Innes for his literary style and Dorothy Sayers as an admirer of her encyclopædic

information? Come, surely you are being inconsistent? In this particular case, a very objectionable, mean old man was shot: he was
very old, and his life was of no value to anybody, so far as can be
judged. I regard the whole thing as a problem—a design, I might
say. The fact that we were at close quarters only renders the interest
more intense, to my way of thinking."

Mackellon put in a word here: "I don't think that Cavenish bothers about the decease of Mr. Albert Folliner, any more than you or
I do. What he dislikes is a police interrogation which involves his
own friends."

Delaunier's regard was quizzical. "His own friends," he repeated
softly. "Well, Cavenish might have rendered Miss Manaton a better
service by persuading her to fall in with her brother's way of thinking. It could have done nobody any harm. The only truth which
matters is truth concerning the murder, and there Miss Manaton
had no evidence to offer. Of what use for that admirable detective
to waste his intelligence pondering over Rosanne's inspection of
the black-out? We could all have told him that it had no bearing on
the facts."

Cavenish flushed and his habitually tranquil face hardened as
he answered: "I said before—and I say it again—to tamper with the
truth is to put yourself in the wrong; it is a fool's game, quite apart
from the ethical aspect. Besides, you forget that Miss Manaton herself would not consider suppressing the truth, either for her own
benefit, or the convenience of other people."

Delaunier shrugged his shoulders, a smile twitching his mobile
lips. "As you will, *mon cher*, as you will. The convenience of other
people, you suggest. The convenience would have been for Miss
Manaton alone—though it might have eased the anxiety of her
brother and her friends. For myself, *cela m'est bien egal.*"

Mackellon interposed here. "You spoke about the detective—Chief Inspector Macdonald—being intelligent. I agree with you there. Any man less like a fool I never met, or less likely to be fooled. I don't think he is likely to make any glaring mistakes, but if he had once discovered that we were tampering with the evidence, he would have been disposed to disbelieve everything we told him."

Delaunier nodded. "Yes, yes. I see your point. Incidentally, have you seen Manaton to-day?"

"Obviously not," said Mackellon. "Cavenish and I have had our jobs to do. The only time we are free is in the evenings. Have you seen him?"

"I have, and he was in a very vile temper. He had said that he wanted to go on with the Richelieu portrait, but when I arrived, ready to pose for his convenience, Bruce says that he does not feel like work. Rosanne was out, else she might have made him see sense. As for his portrait—it can go to the devil. I can't be bothered to go running round after him if he chooses to be temperamental. Well, if I don't see you again before the inquest, I take it we shall be called to give evidence?"

"It depends entirely how far the police have got with their case," said Cavenish. "It's quite probable that the first sitting will be no more than a necessary formality. They will take evidence of identification and of the discovery of death, and then adjourn. None of us has any first-hand evidence to give on the two primary points. They will call Verraby, Neil Folliner, and Mrs. Tubbs—the latter being the last to see the old man alive. Of course we may be summoned to attend in case the Coroner decides to take all the evidence available. I gather that the inquest will be held to-morrow morning, so if we are wanted, we shall get notice to-night. Good-night, Delaunier. Good of you to have looked in."

"Not at all, not at all. Good-night, both of you. Mackellon, remember you have promised me another game some time. Good-night!"

II

After Delaunier had gone, there was silence between the two men, and at length Mackellon said:

"Well, I gather that your previous irritation with that chap has not abated."

"It has not," said Cavenish. "Maybe I'm being unreasonable. One has a tendency to judge people against a background. A man may be acceptable enough in a given set of circumstances, and quite unacceptable in others. Delaunier as a chess player, or as an actor, may be an interesting fellow. When he starts airing his views about the affair of last night, I admit that I don't like him. It's no use making an analogy of a detective story: the two experiences have nothing in common to my way of thinking. How do you feel about it?"

"I'm interested, but in a more impersonal way than yourself," said Mackellon. "What I should like to get at is the opinion and reactions of that C.I.D. fellow. Why did he came into the studio? What did he think of it all? Did he believe any of us, or did he think we were all telling a carefully concocted yarn? He gave me the impression of being unusually aware: not only listening to what was said, but studying the speaker with a cool objective judgment. You know we must have looked a damned funny lot to him. Had that occurred to you?"

Cavenish moved uncomfortably in his chair. "Yes. It occurred to me all right, but I thought the Chief Inspector was an unusually intelligent fellow: he seemed to grasp the situation immediately, without either surprise or incredulity."

"Never batted an eyelid. True to his nationality. He's a Highlander, or derived from them. Incidentally," Mackellon paused here and knocked his pipe out, and started refilling it as he asked:

"Just how much do you know about the Manatons?"

Again there was a silence, and at length Cavenish answered:

"Just about as much as you do—barring a few words Rosanne has let drop, which I shan't repeat."

Mackellon looked at the fire as he smoked, and then he said: "You remember Delaunier asked us to his rooms one evening for a double game of chess. I played Delaunier, you played Manaton. One or two things have occurred to me since. We stayed and jawed round the fire after our games were finished. I thought Manaton was an intelligent fellow in many ways, but he had curious gaps in his information about current events."

"Yes," said Cavenish dryly. "He had. I didn't notice him much at the time. He's a good chess player. That's all I cared about—not so good as Delaunier, of course. That chap's nearly in the front rank. Did it ever occur to you—as it occurred to me—that Delaunier and Manaton together might be going to propose playing for stakes? They didn't, though. Then we went along to the studio one evening, and after I'd got to know Rosanne I gave up criticising her brother."

Cavenish spoke simply, and Mackellon nodded. "Quite. I wish you luck. I still do. I like Rosanne Manaton. I think she's fundamentally straight, and she must have had the hell of a life with that brother of hers: she's honestly devoted to him and she slaves for him, to keep him straight."

"Then you think he's crooked?"

"Not of necessity. He's unstable, and he gets drunk very easily. Not drunk in a noisy tipsy way, but in a way which makes him reckless and absolutely irresponsible. Hasn't he ever borrowed money from you? I thought so. That money would have gone to the nearest pub. He puts down neat whisky as long as his money lasts. I lent him money once, and Rosanne asked me not to do it again." Mackellon got up and stretched his long limbs. "When Macdonald was talking to us in the studio, I had a feeling that he had grasped something of all that without being told a word of it."

"That's an exaggeration, of course," said Cavenish. "The Chief Inspector is a trained observer, and as such he would gather a lot that the average man would miss. As a matter of fact, I thought that Bruce Manaton showed up unusually well when he was talking to Macdonald. He was reasonable and explicit, and courteous—a quality not always noticeable in him."

Mackellon laughed. "Meaning that he is habitually infernally rude. Well, if you don't feel like a game, I'll get off home. I've got some figures I want to check."

"Right." Cavenish got up and stood fiddling with some spills on the mantelpiece. As Mackellon turned to the door, the older man said:

"You haven't said what you came to say, have you?"

Mackellon stood still by the door. "No. I suppose I haven't, actually—but perhaps it's as well to leave some things unsaid. I admit that I wish we had never got to know Delaunier or the Manatons, but I don't suppose you feel like that about it."

"No," said Cavenish quietly. "I don't."

III

After Mackellon had gone, Cavenish took up his book again and tried to read, but found that he could not settle down to it. Having read the same page three times without taking in a word of the meaning, he put the book down and decided to go for a walk and try to get rid of the unaccustomed restlessness which possessed him.

He put on his overcoat and went quietly out of the house. It was a black moonless night, and he stood at the front door until his eyes grew a little accustomed to the dark. As he stood, Cavenish felt a sudden sense of unease. He had only the vaguest notions about police procedure, and he wondered if he and Mackellon and Delaunier were all being "shadowed." Were the police watching their movements, noting that the three of them had foregathered this evening for a consultation? Some motive of caution in Cavenish's careful, sensible mind told him that he would be better advised to go indoors again, rather than roam the streets in the black-out. The thought irritated him and he stepped out, determined to walk off the malaise which possessed him.

When he reached the main road he turned northwards, towards Hampstead. The air was clear to-night, and a sharp north wind met him: he could see the traffic lights at the road junctions ahead— Circus Road and Marlborough Place—the green lights shining beneath their hoods with startling vividness. There was very little traffic on the wide road, and still fewer pedestrians. Now that his eyes were accustomed to the gloom, Cavenish set out at a good pace, finding that the exercise lulled his sense of discomfort. When he reached Swiss Cottage, he hesitated at the junction of the roads, and then took the right-hand fork, leading to Fitzjohn's Avenue and the Heath. As he began to mount the long hill, he admitted to himself that he knew where he was going. Common sense might bid him keep away, but something stronger than common sense was urging him in the direction of Hollyberry Hill.

Cavenish, as Rosanne Manaton knew, was a poet at heart. Beneath the façade of organising ability and conscientious industry was a mind which played with the music of words, and as he walked his mind repeated the rhythm and melody of one of the most melodious of poets. Asked for his opinion of Swinburne, Cavenish would have said: "It's all sound, just skilful sound, without any significant thought behind it," but as he strode up the hill his mind took pleasure in the rhythm of "Atalanta."

> "Where shall we find her, how shall we sing to her,
> Fold our hands round her knees and sing;
> Oh that man's heart were as fire and could spring to her,
> Fire, and the strength of the streams that spring."

His mind was too occupied with the verse to be analytical, and no errant sense of the ludicrous prompted him to laugh at the thought of a middle-aged, conscientious Home Office official striding up Fitzjohn's Avenue in the black-out to the lilting music of Swinburne.

Towards the top of the hill he turned off to the right and made his way through several small roads until he reached Hollyberry Hill and turned in at the gate of number twenty-five towards the studio. Even at the door he hesitated, and then, angry with his own hesitation, knocked at the studio door. It was opened by Bruce Manaton; heedless of the black-out regulations, he threw the unscreened door wide, so that Cavenish was confused by the sudden glare of light.

"Damn you, what do you want? Where's Rosanne?" demanded the painter. "Where is she, I ask you?"

IV

Cavenish pushed inside and closed the studio door. Facing him, at the far end, was the great white canvas with the drawing of the Cardinal. The canvas was streaked now with daubs of violent red, vermilion, cadmium scarlet, alizarin crimson and cobalt violet shadows. To Cavenish it looked quite mad—experiment or lunacy, he knew not which.

"Where is she?" demanded Manaton again. He had donned his blue painter's coat, and his palette was still in his left hand, bedaubed with thick shining splodges of red.

"I don't know where she is, Manaton. How should I know? I haven't seen Rosanne since I left here last night. You'd better tell me what you mean."

"She went out, just after tea, to do the shopping, she said. That man was here—Macdonald. He's searched the place, ransacked everything. Rosanne went out just before he started: she knew he was going to search—and she's not come back. God! I shall go mad if I don't know where she is."

"Didn't she say where she was going, or when she'd be in?"

"No, I tell you. She just went."

"If you're really worried about her, why not tell the police? They'll know if there's been an accident."

Manaton flung his palette down and laughed, a furious sound with no mirth in it.

"Police!" he stormed. "Are you being funny? For all I know the police have taken her. It's just the sort of fool-thing they would do. I tell you I *can't* tell the police. I don't know where she is, or what she's doing or why..." He stamped his feet furiously, and shouted, "As for you, damn and blast you, if it hadn't been for you this needn't have

happened. You and your puritanical conscience, you poor codfish—
you knew *you* were safe enough. If you'd told Rosanne to say she was
in here, with us, this would never have happened. It's your fault."

Cavenish stood aghast, not knowing what to reply.

"You're wrong," he protested. "I know you're wrong. You wanted
to shield Rosanne with lies—"

"Yes, damn you! I wanted to shield her, with lies or with anything else. Don't I know what she's done for me? Is there anything I
wouldn't do for her? You make me sick, you and your prating ways.
Get out, I say! Get out!"

"I tell you I *won't* get out! I want to know where Rosanne is…"

His words were interrupted by Manaton's storm of laughter.

"Where she is? She's not here, I tell you that! Didn't Macdonald
go over the place inch by inch? Ask him! She's not here. Go and ask
Delaunier! Perhaps he knows."

Robert Cavenish felt helpless: helpless and sick at heart. To
stay here was useless. He went outside and began to tramp up and
down the dark roadway, thinking, arguing with himself, helpless
and irresolute.

CHAPTER TWELVE

I

REEVES, HAVING BEEN GIVEN THE JOB OF FINDING THE EX-tenant of the Manatons' studio, decided to call on Miss Stanton of Sedgemoor Avenue as a start. Reeves wanted to find out what Mr. Randall Stort looked like, and he guessed that Miss Stanton was an observant person.

He rang the bell at the very superior front door of Ithaca, belabouring his brains in the endeavour to remember where he had heard the name Ithaca before. "One of those yarns… argonauts or something…" was as far as he had progressed when the front door was opened to him by "the holy terror" in person. She was dressed in a severe tailor-made suit, her white hair brushed back hard against her head, and she now wore horn-rimmed glasses, which made her look still more awe-inspiring. Reeves spoke with becoming humility.

"Good-afternoon, madam. Could you spare me a few minutes to answer some questions? I hope it is not inconvenient."

"Not at all. I am never too busy to do my duty," boomed Miss Stanton. "Come in. I was just about to have tea. The tea is already made, so I can offer you a cup during your interrogation."

"Very kind of you, ma'am," said Reeves.

He rubbed his shoes vigorously on the doormat before risking a step on the mirror-like surface of the hall floor; he hoped he would not slip on it. For some reason, Miss Stanton had succeeded in making a very competent young detective inspector feel like a small boy again.

"Come in. Sit down."

Miss Stanton knew her own mind clearly. She led the way into an old-fashioned dining-room whose solid mahogany shone with polish. A lace-edged cloth covered one end of the long table and tea was laid upon it for one person. Miss Stanton fetched another cup and saucer and plate from the sideboard, sat down at the head of the table and seized the silver teapot, saying:

"Well, young man, what do you want to know? Help yourself to toast."

"Thank you," said Reeves, continuing immediately, in a subdued version of the voice in which he gave evidence in court. "I want to know what Mr. Randall Stort looked like—the previous tenant of the studio abutting on your garden."

Miss Stanton said "Ha!" in a deep, victorious tone of voice, as she passed Reeves a cup of very hot, very strong tea, to which she had added sugar. (The tea was exactly as Reeves liked it, and the toast was excellent.)

"I'm delighted to know that someone is expending a little intelligence over this deplorable crime," said Miss Stanton. "Mr. Randall Stort is a tall man, inclined to obesity, with an unhealthy, pale face, lank black hair which falls in a lock over his forehead like the archfiend's own, and dark eyes. I should say that he is about fifty years of age. He has a birthmark on his neck below his right ear, and he is left-handed. I can tell you all these details because I called upon him in his studio to tell him what I thought of his behaviour in trespassing on my property. Believe me, I did not mince my words. I have the satisfaction of knowing that one woman, at least, has told him exactly what she thought of him."

There was a triumphant gleam in Miss Stanton's eye, and Reeves chuckled inwardly.

"Very courageous of you, madam—and your accurate description will be very valuable. Do you know anything more about Mr. Stort, or Mr. Listelle, who lived with him?"

"I know what was current gossip throughout the neighbourhood," she replied. "Unfortunately, with so many people having been frightened out of London by the air raids, there are not many left to confirm what I say. I can only assure you that I have an accurate memory, and that I do not approve of malicious gossip. During the latter part of Mr. Stort's tenancy of the studio—before the raids started, however—a woman lived on the ground floor of number twenty-five Hollyberry Hill. I think it probable—as did other people—that she was Stort's mistress. I know that he used to climb into her room direct from the studio; I have seen him do it. He was constantly in the house, they made no attempt to conceal their intimacy. Can you wonder that I wished to have a trellis to raise my wall?" she concluded indignantly.

"Indeed, no, madam," said Reeves. He went on, "Did you know anything about Mr. Folliner himself?"

"No, nothing of any interest. He had lived in that house for many years, during which period his house, and those on either side of it, deteriorated steadily. I am told that he was very poor, but if that was so, I fail to understand why he did not sell his house. It was a freehold property, and before the war he could have sold it for a good sum. Will you have another cup of tea?" she ended.

"Thank you very much, ma'am," said Reeves sedately, and then continued: "We are anxious to trace Mr. Stort, and to find out where he is living now—if he is still living, that is."

"Oh, dear me, yes, he is still living," replied Miss Stanton with animation. "I am sure of that." She got up and went to a paper rack in the corner of the room, and returned with a copy of the *Morning*

Mail. She pointed to a small cartoon in the corner of the paper. "You notice that the picture is signed with a hieroglyphic resembling 'Rand' and a long squiggle. That stands, I think, for Randall, but the point is that that signature is Stort's. I told you that I went into his studio. His drawings were pinned out on a board—not small drawings like that, but very big ones, done in dashing bold lines. Evidently his drawings are reduced for publication. I saw the signature, and it is unmistakable. I admit the work is clever; coarse, perhaps, but vigorous—rather like Stort himself."

"Miss Stanton, madam," said Reeves, "you're a perfect marvel! I can't begin to tell you how grateful I am to you."

"Good gracious—and why, might I ask?" she demanded.

"Because you've saved me a week of weary, boring, irritating work," said Reeves. "If it hadn't been for you, and your very remarkable powers of accurate observation, I should probably have gone trailing round from Bickford's offices to some derelict country cottage, and on and on until the trail petered out. You see," he went on, "we've nothing at all against Stort—nothing. We want to find him and to interrogate him, but if, by any chance, he's done anything he shouldn't have, he's probably changed his name and it won't be easy to find him, *but*, with the information you have given me, I ought to be able to run him down in two twos."

"Good gracious!" replied Miss Stanton, "you surprise me! I am very gratified to think that I can be of assistance. I hope also that you will not let Mr. Stort outwit you as he outwitted your colleagues in this neighbourhood," she added severely. "He made a habit of using my garden as a short cut to his studio. I have *seen* him doing it—always very late at night. I complained to the police about this, and Mr. Stort, of course, denied it. The police made some efforts,

I believe, to catch him trespassing—but of course they never succeeded. He was much too clever for them."

"I'll promise you that he doesn't outwit me, madam," said Reeves, adding, "though if I *do* get on his trail fast enough for him to be of any use, it will be thanks to you entirely. And thank you very much for the delicious tea," he went on. "I've never enjoyed a cup more. I hope that one day you will show me your Christmas roses."

"Ah, my Hellebore," she said proudly. "Come this way."

Reeves was led into the drawing-room at the back of the house, and shown a small glass bowl where half a dozen flat white flowers rested among their handsome green leaves. Miss Stanton regarded them with an air of almost maternal delight.

"I'm so glad you like them," she said. "So few people know anything about flowers."

II

Less than half an hour later Reeves was at the offices of the *Morning Mail* in Fleet Street. He saw the business editor, and was then passed on to the art editor, a man named Brenling. To this gentleman—busy, as all Fleet Street is busy—Reeves said:

"I want the address of an artist of yours—Randall Stort."

"Never heard of him."

Reeves picked up a current issue of the paper and pointed out the cartoon. "The chap who drew this," he said.

"Oh, him. His name's not Stort. He's Victor Rand. What do you want him for?"

"I want his address," said Reeves patiently.

"I don't know his address. I'm busy, anyway. Hi! Miss Blake. Find the officer Rand's address."

"I haven't got his address," replied Miss Blake. "He just sends his stuff in, or brings it in, and collects his money at intervals. I don't know about that. You'd better try the accountant's office. He ought to have an address of some kind—the Inland Revenue people are always wanting addresses."

Reeves went to the accountant's office.

"Victor Rand? Oh, he's always changing his address, I just can't keep pace with him. Funny thing, another fellow was asking for his address to-day. Try this. Westways, Wealden Road, Harrow. That was the last address he gave me."

"Do you know him—by sight?"

"Yes, dark fellow with a face like a potato, and a black lock of hair. Rather a mess." The girl clerk looked up at Reeves. "'Tec, aren't you? What do you want him for?"

"Just for a chat. Who was the other chap who wanted Rand's address?"

"Search me. I don't know. I've got a spot of work to do sometimes. The other chap didn't get his address if that's what you want to know."

III

It was six o'clock when Reeves came out of the *Morning Mail* offices. He went into a telephone box and reported to Scotland Yard and then made his way to Baker Street and took the Metropolitan Railway to Harrow. Harrow covers a large area, and Reeves knew better than to go wandering round in the black-out hunting for an obscure house in an unknown road. He telephoned to his nearest colleagues of the Metropolitan Police, and was soon in a police car which drove him a very long way and put him down at the corner of a little dark roadway.

"Fourth house on the right," said his guide. "I'll wait until you're inside and then stand by."

Reeves could just make out the shapes of the small suburban houses on either side: a very unpretentious road of mass-produced modern houses, semi-detached, all replicas of one another.

The fourth house on the right—"Westways"—showed a thin façade of white rough cast and windows of unadulterated blackness. No least tiny glow of curtained light encouraged a visitor to believe that there was any life within to respond to a summons at the small front door. Reeves knocked—not too peremptorily, a carefully calculated unofficial knock. There was no response so far as the front door was concerned, but the thinly-built house enabled the detective's quick ears to learn that someone was at home. He knocked again. After a further wait, the door was opened, and a woman's voice, emerging from an almost dark passage, asked,

"Well? Who do you want?"

The voice was apprehensive and bad-tempered, and Reeves planned his campaign accordingly.

"I want Mr. Victor Rand. I've just come from the *Morning Mail* offices."

"Oh, damn, didn't he send that stuff in? I reminded him. Said he'd take it to-day."

"He must have forgotten," said Reeves. "Is he at home?"

"At home?—at seven o'clock in the evening? What a hope. Oh, come in, it's too cold to stand talking at the door."

Reeves took a couple of steps forward and stood and waited while the door was shut behind him and a light switch put down. He could then see the woman who had admitted him. She was quite young, but thin and weary looking, clad in a tight-fitting scarlet jumper and navy blue slacks. Her fair hair, once elaborately set in modish curls was tousled now, as though she had just got up, and the scarlet of her lipstick made her face look the whiter.

"Isn't he the limit?" she grumbled. "That's the only job he's got, and he can't take the trouble to see that his stuff goes in at the right time. Come along in."

Reeves followed her down the passage to a room at the back of the house and she put down a switch which brought on a strong white light whose glare made Reeves blink after the previous dimness. The room was much larger than he would have expected from the size of the house—it must have occupied nearly the whole ground floor. The walls were distempered in white, and there were drawings on them, some in charcoal, some in colour—bold vigorous portraits. The faces all had something of the same quality, staring, avid faces, harsh and mocking.

"Oh, don't look at them, they give me the pip," said the girl. "His *Mail* drawings were in one of those rolls—cardboard rolls. We ought to be able to find them somewhere. God, what a muck he gets the place in... Got a fag on you?"

Reeves produced a packet of Player's and gave them to her.

"Oh, ta. Decent of you. I'm broke, and the old hag won't give me any more tick. He *is* the limit," she went on complainingly. "He's clever enough—look at all this stuff. Other chaps make money, chaps without half his brains. My hat, if *I* could do it—draw like that—I'd make money out of it somehow."

She sat down on a divan against one of the walls, lolling back and kicking off piles of loose sheets on to the bare floor-boards. There was very little furniture in the room—a draughtsman's desk covered with a litter of materials, newspapers and magazines, cigarette ash and some dirty plates; a couple of chairs, an easel, a model's platform and stacks of old canvases and portfolios.

"I know it's a muck," said the girl, as she inhaled her cigarette smoke avidly. "I tried to keep it decent when we came but I got fed-up, disheartened. I'd get some work myself, only I've been ill. When I'm better I'm going into the Services. Anything's better than this."

Reeves nodded. "Yes. I'd say it was. I can't see that roll you were talking about. D'you know what time he'll be in?"

"Oh, any old time. Depends if he can get people to stand him drinks: he won't come back here while he can get a bit of fun somewhere else. I say, if you find those drawings, can you leave the money for them?"

"No. I'm afraid I can't. It has to go through the office."

Reeves was aware that his own position at the moment was irregular. According to regulations he should have had another officer with him—but Reeves did not always conform to regulations. He went on:

"Do you mind if I look at some of those canvases? I'm interested in pictures. Some of them might be worth something."

"Lord, yes! Look at them all! Boy, if you'd only buy one I might get some supper."

Reeves looked at her. "Bad as that, is it? Well, it ought to run to the price of supper."

He began tilting back the canvases, one by one. They were mostly portraits, generally unfinished. At the back, against the wall, was

a larger canvas: after a glance down at it, Reeves pulled it out, and
stood it up against the table. "Lord, that's clever!" he said.

Clever it certainly was. The canvas depicted a very old man,
whose pallid skin was stretched taut over his bald bony cranium
and hawk-like nose. His eyes were set far back in the heavy
shadows of deep orbital ridges, and his thin lips were sucked in
to a hard line which yet achieved a grin. The head was painted
in such a manner that the structure of the skull beneath the
parchment-like skin showed clear and hard. The eyes glittered in
their deep sockets, and the claw-like hands were holding some
crisp white papers—five-pound notes. Reeves stared fascinated
at the canvas. The old man was sitting up in bed and behind his
head was the corner of a brass and iron bedstead. There was a
cash-box on his knees, and the patchwork quilt on the bed was that
which Reeves had seen on Mr. Folliner's bed: the brass knobs and
elaborations of the bedpost were the same too. Beside the cash-
box lay a pistol. The title given to the rather ghastly *tour-de-force*
was "Peep-Show."

The girl lolling on the divan looked at Reeves with calculating
eyes. "Yes, it's clever, isn't it?" she echoed. "It must be worth a lot,
only people won't pay for pictures these days. I believe if it was
shown at a decent exhibition it might bring in a lot of money. It'd
be worth anybody's while to buy it."

Reeves was doing some quick thinking: beneath his detective
instinct and clear, hard, thinking capacity was the essential humanity
which had made him sweat and toil in an inferno of blazing ruins to
rescue his fellow-creatures in the blitz. He turned to the girl.

"Look here, kid. Are you married to him?"

She did not resent the question. Reeves guessed that she was too
hungry to resent anything which might lead to a meal.

"No, thanks be," she replied. "I was potty on him for a bit, but I'm through with that. Who're you, anyway?"

"C.I.D. I'm on duty."

"God! What's he done?"

"I don't know that he's done anything. I want to ask him some questions. If you'll answer one question yourself, perhaps you can save a lot of trouble. Look here, I've got my mate outside, another officer. I'll get him in if you like, so that you can have a witness and know I'm playing fair. I don't want to get you mixed up in a mess if I haven't got to."

The stark fear which had shone in her eyes for a minute died down, and she answered, "Oh, get on with your questions. I don't mind you. You're a decent sort. I don't believe he's done anything awful. He's too lazy, and he's a funk, anyway. He'd never risk doing anything tough—he'd rather live on a girl like me. What d'you want to know?"

"How long have you lived with him?"

"About a year now. This was my home—I paid the rent. Only I've been ill."

"What's your name?"

"Jenny Lane."

"Do you know what Victor Rand—if that's what he calls himself—was doing yesterday evening between eight o'clock and nine?"

"Yes. He was here. It was foggy, and he was too lazy to go out. He had a couple of other chaps here—boys in the Air Force. He drew their pictures, and they brought a bottle of gin with them. It was all gone before they left."

"That's all right then," said Reeves. "If he can prove he was here he's got nothing to worry about. It's just a matter of asking him a few questions. Where was he living when you first took up with him?"

"In the country somewhere. I picked him up in Brighton. He'd done a bunk out of London because of the raids—he funked it. After a bit the country got him down, and he wanted to get back to London again. So did I. I'd got a bit of money, and we came here. It was my aunt's house once. We've just mucked along—and then I got ill, and it was a proper old mess-up. I'm about through with it, I tell you straight. Funny, the way I'm talking to you. Haven't talked like this for years—but I'm fed-up. He went out, and he pinched my last ten-bob note before he went. Makes a girl see red, that does."

Reeves nodded. "Yes. A dirty trick. If I give you another ten-bob note, can you get a meal anywhere hereabouts?"

"Lord, yes. There's a pub round the corner where they'll always give you a snack. Will you come, too?"

"No. I've got to stay here and see Rand when he comes in. Does he always call himself Rand?"

"Signs his drawings like that. It isn't his name. His name's Stort. He's got that name on his identity card—it's his real name, the other's only a professional name."

"Have you ever heard him talk about a studio he had in Hampstead?"

"Oh, I've heard him talk about lots of places, all very fine and large. Studios in Paris and Chelsea, and all that. Mind you, he's clever—I'm not saying he isn't, but he's bone lazy. I think he did quite well before the war, but people won't buy pictures now, and there's the paper shortage, and there you are."

"Just one more question," said Reeves. "Has Rand ever mentioned a fellow called Listelle?"

"Oh, him! I nearly died laughing about him. He was afraid of bombs—frightened stiff he was. He went right away from London into the country and lived in a cottage miles from anywhere and a

Jerry just jettisoned all his bombs one night plonk on that cottage and that was the end of Listelle—died of fright, as you might say."

"I've heard of more than one person died of running away," said Reeves. "Well, look here, kid, you'd better go and get some supper—you look hungry—but don't go and mix your drinks, and don't ever tell anyone I gave you a ten-bob note, or I shall get into no end of a howling row."

"I won't split. Boy, you are a decent good sort! Do you know I haven't had a meal to-day?"

"You look like it," said Reeves gruffly. "You're no advertisement for your boy friend."

Jenny Lane pulled a coat round her thin shoulders.

"You going to stay here? He won't be in yet, not until eleven o'clock, anyway, but if he does come, don't go and tell him that you told me you were a cop. He'll think I put you on to him. Anyway, I'll be back in half an hour."

Two minutes after Jenny Lane had let herself out of the house, Reeves followed her into the road, and found his reliable colleague waiting patiently a few yards away.

"Go after that kid and keep your eye on her, mate," said Reeves. "She said she was going to a pub to get some supper. If she tries doing a bunk, bring her back here. She may go and try to warn her boy friend I'm here, and she mustn't do that."

"Can do," replied the other promptly and set off after Jenny Lane.

Reeves went back into the house. He wanted to make sure that that picture was safe: whatever happened, he must have that picture. While he waited, he looked carefully through the remaining canvases and the portfolios, and took out one or two sketches which interested him. He wished that there were a telephone in the house: he wanted to report to Macdonald.

To pass the time, he sat down and wrote up his official report in his notebook, and by the time he had finished that Jenny Lane came back.

"I feel a different girl," she said. "Sausage and chips and apple pudding—a real blow out. I got you another packet of gaspers."

Reeves grinned. "Thanks. That was thoughtful of you. Glad you had a good supper."

She yawned. "Life's funny, isn't it? I've never been treated to supper by a copper before. I've known some decent ones though. When in doubt, ask a policeman. I'm sleepy. I think I'll go to bed. When he comes in, you can give him the same dope as you gave me—say you come from the *Morning Mail* office. You've got a nerve, haven't you, telling whackers like that."

"It wasn't a whacker. It was true," retorted Reeves. "I left the *Morning Mail* office at six-thirty and came straight here. It was your own idea that I'd come to fetch his drawings."

"Well, I don't care a damn anyway. I'm through. I'm going to clear out in the morning." She yawned again. "Lord, I'm sleepy."

"All right. Trot off to bed," said Reeves. "Just tell me two things before you go, though. Is this drawing a portrait of Stort?"

"Yes, that's him—just like him, too. He loves making self-portraits, as he calls them. Lord knows why. He's no beauty chorus."

"He's no illusions on that score, anyway," said Reeves, grinning at the uncompromising portrait. "Next, when he spends his evenings in town, does he go to any particular joint, or just roll round promiscuous like?"

"He's an expert on pubs, I tell you straight. He says there isn't a pub in the four-mile radius he doesn't know. One place he's always going to though is that café close to the Coliseum—a snack bar it is really, the Flamingo. A rum lot go there, actors and artists and press men and all the rest."

"I know it," said Reeves. "Well, you toddle off—and take a word of advice. Clear out of this and get a decent job You ought to have more sense than to live with a fellow like this."

"A girl's got to live, hasn't she?"

"Call it living? I don't."

"Oh, I dunno. Thanks for my supper. Saved my life, that did."

Jenny Lane went upstairs and Reeves shrugged his shoulders. In his policeman's career he had seen many like her, and with the practical common sense which was his chief essential Reeves thought it a pity that any girl should be such a fool: he hated untidiness and squalor and what he called "muckery."

He went outside again and found the sergeant.

"O.K.?" demanded the latter. "That girl was hungry—no mistake about that."

"She's not hungry now," said Reeves. "Can you 'phone this message through to C.O. for me, and come back and tell me if there's any further orders. I reckon I'd better stand by until Stort comes back here. Don't want to miss him."

"O.K. I'll go along to our box—it's only a few minutes' run along the main road. Then I'll come back here and report."

Reeves went inside again and sat down to wait. His mind turned to supper. He could have done with sausages and chips himself... and beer. It was just after half-past nine. He sat and smoked, thinking over the case, musing over the drawings on the wall in front of him, and recalling the smudged-out frescoes on the walls of old Folliner's drawing-room. He put together the odd pieces of evidence he had collected, together with all the details given in Macdonald's report—a jig-saw pattern, in which the pieces could be dovetailed.

At ten o'clock a cautious knock sounded at the front door. Reeves went and opened it.

"Better let me come in," said the sergeant.

Reeves led him into the brightly lighted room and the sergeant's eyes goggled as he saw the wall paintings. "Blimey!" he said, and then turned to Reeves very soberly.

"Sorry, mate, I'm afraid it's no go. They picked Stort up off the live rail just outside the station. He must have got out of the train on the wrong side, and fallen on his head. Our chaps reported to C.O."

"Damn!" said Reeves, and the other replied,

"Sorry, old chap, but it wasn't your fault. You're to get outside a meal and then report to the chap on duty at the corner of Hollyberry Hill."

Reeves stood still, his face utterly despondent. He remembered saying to Miss Stanton, "I'll promise you he doesn't outwit me, madam."

Reeves felt that he had been outwitted, all the same.

CHAPTER THIRTEEN

I

AFTER MACDONALD HAD LEFT THE STUDIO, HIS SEARCH COMpleted, he went back to Scotland Yard and heard the report of Detective Ward, who had been spending his day enquiring into the ownership of property in Hollyberry Hill, and also picking up any local gossip and general information. He had not neglected to have a pint at "the local," and had actually been in the Hollyberry Tavern when Delaunier was acquiring such information as the topers of the neighbourhood could dispense. Ward, with his very large spectacles and rather stupid stare, sat on a stool in silence, ignored by the animated company. After Delaunier had gone, Ward asked for another pint, saying timidly:

"I gather you've been having some trouble around here."

"Call it trouble if you like: plain murder's the name of it," replied the landlord.

Another voice put in: "All comes of a miser 'oarding his money like that. Asking for it, I says. Why didn't 'e put it in War Savings, same's anyone else."

"And how do you know he *was* a miser?" demanded another voice. "There's all this talk, and it seems to me it's just rumour—baseless rumour. The poor old chap was always starving, I'm told. Who first put it round that he *was* a miser? I reckon they've got a lot to be responsible for."

"That's plain sense, that is," volunteered another. "Now then, old friend," turning to the landlord. "Who first told *you* old Folliner was a miser?"

The landlord looked somewhat nonplussed. "Who first told me?" he asked. "Well, I don't know, I'm sure. A lot of people have said so. The old man was always known as a very hard old customer—drove a hard bargain. He was well off at one time, too. Old Jenks, who used to sweep the crossing up there before he went into the workhouse, old Jenks used to say he remembered Mr. Folliner in a top hat and tail coat once. Then he got shabbier and shabbier, until his soles nearly parted company with his uppers, and he gave up going out at all. Then look at his house, and the shocking state it's in! Not been painted since the last war."

Ward spoke timidly: "Doesn't that prove that he was very poor—not of necessity a miser?"

The landlord scratched his head, and somebody else said: "I'll tell you who started this miser talk: it was those fellows in the studio—not the ones who're there now, the ones who ran away when the bombing started."

"Ar... r," said the landlord, "that's right, that is. That little chap with a foreign name. A rare one to talk, he was. I remember he said when it was quiet in the studio he could hear the chink of coins in the house when the old man counted them of an evening."

"That's a damned whopper, anyway," put in someone else. "Do you expect anyone to believe a yarn like that?"

A gentle voice spoke next: the voice of a quiet old gentleman who sat in a corner by the fire. "Mr. Folliner was very old," he said "*very* old; that's the trouble. You're all too young to remember. I'm seventy-five years old now. When I was a young man, Mr. Folliner lived in that same house... say fifty years ago." The soft voice trailed off, but Ward moved over to the old man's corner and spoke to him.

"I was interested in what you were saying, sir," he said. "You really remember this neighbourhood fifty years ago?"

"Yes. Yes. I remember those days much better than I remember last week. Fifty years ago... 1893, before the Jubilee... well, well. I was in my father's business—he was a pharmaceutical chemist. Mr. Folliner got married, and he brought his bride to live in that house. He would have been aged forty or thereabouts, but he looked older. He was always a hard man. She was a young thing, very young, a beautiful girl. People talked. It was said she had been an actress—a terrible stigma in those days. I don't know. My mother was interested in the poor young thing: she had a baby, and then she ran away and took the baby with her. There was a lot of talk at the time... Mr. Folliner had always been a harsh man, but after that he grew meaner and grimmer. He was said to care about nothing but money. That's why it came to be said that he was a miser... talk grows, like a snowball."

Ward leaned forward. "Wasn't the wife ever heard of again, sir?—or the child? Was it a girl, or a boy?"

"It was a boy, my mother saw it. We never heard of the wife again, but one day some time before the last war, in 1913 I think, a very handsome young fellow came into my shop and asked if I knew the address of a Mr. Folliner... thirty years ago... it seems like yesterday. I was certain that young man was Mr. Folliner's son, there was just a look of him..."

"Time, gentlemen, time!" cried the landlord.

Ward managed to step outside just behind the old man.

"I have enjoyed hearing you talk, sir," he said. "I hope to see you again."

"Any day: any day. I come in for my modest half-pint," replied the old gentleman. He walked away, tapping the railings with his stick. Somebody nudged Ward's arm.

"Poor old chap. He's almost blind. Comes in here every day and toddles back round the corner all by himself."

"Blind?" said Ward. "What a pity."

"Ay. That's a pitiful thing, that is," replied the other.

II

After Macdonald had heard the full report of Ward's researches, he had a quick supper and then went out to Hampstead again, and called on Mr. Lewis Verraby. Verraby was sitting in the same handsome panelled room, and he greeted Macdonald with effusion.

"Delighted to see you, Chief Inspector. Delighted. How goes your case?"

"We are still piecing information together, sir: the case is by no means complete. In the light of certain facts which have been established, I have come to give you an opportunity of reconsidering some of your own evidence."

"*My own evidence?*" Verraby stared at Macdonald: tried indeed to stare the other man down. With heightened colour and bulging eyes Verraby enquired:

"May I ask precisely what you mean?"

"Yes, sir. You stated that when you entered Mr. Folliner's house, you went upstairs, opened the bedroom door, and found the soldier, whom you arrested, already in the bedroom, at the bedside. I don't think that statement is correct."

"Indeed! Am I to understand, Chief Inspector, that you are accepting the word of the arrested man in preference to my own?"

"No, sir. In detection it is not word against word, but fact against fact, which is decisive. One of the first things done by my department on arrival at deceased's house was to take photographs of the floor, in the entrance hall, on the stairs, and in the bedroom. Your own footmarks were easily identified. From these photographs we have evidence that you went up the stairs *before* Neil Folliner did. His footmarks are superimposed on your own."

There was a dead silence. Verraby's colour had faded, and his face was almost grey, but he still tried to bluster.

"Your reading of those photographs must be at fault, Chief Inspector."

"No, sir. There is no possibility of mistake, but the final verdict on the photographs will not be mine. They will be put into court as evidence. In view of this—and other facts—I give you the opportunity of reconsidering your statement. You understand, however, that it is my duty to caution you that anything you say can be taken down in writing and used as evidence. You are not under any obligation to make a statement, but if you wish to make an explanation you now have the opportunity of doing so."

"This," cried Mr. Verraby, "is inconceivable! Do you mean to say that you are accusing *me* of murder?"

"No, sir. I am a detective and I am seeking evidence. I am perfectly willing to tell you some of the evidence collected by my department during the course of the day. It is known to us that you are the chief member of a syndicate which has been buying property in this neighbourhood. You—or your syndicate—own the houses comprising that block in Hollyberry Hill in which number 25 is situated—but you do not own number 25, though you have been trying to purchase it for some time." Macdonald paused here, but Verraby said nothing. He simply stared. Macdonald continued: "You admitted, very frankly, yesterday evening that a financier whose capital is tied up in land which he can not develop is in a very embarrassing position. Further, I know that another syndicate would relieve you of your present difficulties if you could offer the entire block in Hollyberry Hill for sale—including number twenty-five."

"My God!" burst out the other, "and on grounds such as that you accuse me of murder?"

"No, sir. I have accused you of nothing. I have asked you for an explanation of a discrepancy in your evidence."

Macdonald paused again, and then continued in exactly the same even voice:

"You, who know a little of police procedure, will understand very well that it is known how often your duty as a special constable took you past Mr. Folliner's house: that you have inspected that house with something more than the attention required by your duty as a constable. Come, sir! Pull yourself together! I have asked you for an explanation."

Mr. Verraby was deflated by this time: so completely deflated that he sat with his head in his hands, his shoulders shaking. Macdonald's incisive voice in his last words was a measure of the disgust he felt with the man before him.

"All you say is true in substance, but it is utterly misleading," groaned Mr. Verraby. "I am guiltless… you must believe that… I am the victim of circumstances. This appalling thing overwhelms me."

"I have no time to waste, sir," said Macdonald sharply. "Once again, I offer you a chance of restating your evidence, and I caution you that it will be inadvisable to make any statement which is not precisely in accordance with facts."

Mr. Verraby sat up—he reminded Macdonald of a deflated frog. "The facts are almost entirely as I stated," he said. "You can understand the difficulties of my position. It is quite true that I have been facing considerable financial embarrassment caused largely by the obstinacy and greed of Mr. Folliner." At this juncture he caught Macdonald's eye and changed his tone to one of pathos. "I was on duty as you know. I patrolled according to regulations, and as I repassed number 25 I saw that the front door was open."

"Did you examine the front door of every house on your beat?" asked Macdonald, and Mr. Verraby hesitated. Then, with a gesture of hopelessness he spread out his hands.

"No, Chief Inspector—but put yourself in my place. That house was associated in my mind with my present troubles. It was becoming an obsession to me..."

Macdonald cut in here: "I should hardly use that expression to a jury," he said. "It is better to state your facts simply. While you had not examined other houses on your beat, you turned your torch light on to the door of Mr. Folliner's house and found it open."

"Exactly. I was puzzled. I went indoors to investigate. The house was perfectly quiet. I went up the stairs—"

"You had been in the house to see Mr. Folliner on previous occasions?" Macdonald's question was uttered in a voice which was more that of a statement than a question.

"Yes... yes. I had tried to reason with him. The light was on in the bedroom, I saw it under the door, as I told you. I opened the door... and I saw the old man lying there... dead. You cannot imagine the horror which possessed me... the fear in my mind. I foresaw what conclusions would be drawn... the danger I was in—I, who was innocent of any complicity, I, who had no knowledge of this dastardly deed—"

"If you confine yourself to facts we shall get on more quickly," said Macdonald.

Verraby drew a long trembling sigh. His eye dwelt longingly on the whisky decanter, but he made no move towards it. "I can only tell you that I was bowled over—completely bowled over," he said. "I felt that I must get away from this horror. I went out of the bedroom and closed the door, and just at that moment I heard sounds downstairs. I realised, in a flash, that the murderer was still in the house."

Macdonald looked at the other with an expression very far removed from sympathy.

"You heard someone else entering the house," he said. "It is not necessary for either of us to analyse your feelings at this juncture. Your subsequent behaviour was sufficiently enlightening."

"You do me an injustice," complained Mr. Verraby. "The one thought in my mind was 'Here is the murderer. I must apprehend him.' I hid behind a door in the landing and waited. The newcomer went into the bedroom—and the rest you know." He leaned forward with his head in his hands, trembling, a wretched figure of a man.

"You evidently expect my sympathy, sir," said Macdonald. "I speak for myself in saying that I do not consider that your case merits any sympathy at all. Because you were afraid of being accused of murder, you used your authority as a Special Constable to accuse another man of a crime which you must have known that he did not commit. In charging Neil Folliner with this crime you misrepresented the evidence. It is plain that on the evidence I should be justified in arresting and charging you with murder."

"But I am innocent! I swear before God that I know nothing of this thing. He was dead before I entered the room. I tell you, I *discovered* this murder: *someone* shot the old man. Isn't it in the highest degree probable that his nephew did so, hoping to inherit the old man's fortune?"

"All this will have to be debated by the jury," said Macdonald. "When you are called as witness at the inquest I advise you to state all facts plainly and accurately. Meantime, though I am not putting you under arrest, I warn you that you must not leave this house."

Mr. Verraby stared at the C.I.D. man with a glance in which horror and incredulity were combined.

"I tell you I did not do it," he wailed—but Macdonald made no answer.

CHAPTER FOURTEEN

I

WHEN MACDONALD LEFT MR. VERRABY'S HOUSE HE MADE his way back on foot to Hollyberry Hill, and he arrived there just as Robert Cavenish turned into number twenty-five and knocked at the door of the studio. Macdonald heard Bruce Manaton's outburst when he opened the door, and the Chief Inspector walked silently down the side of the studio and stood by the small window below the north light, whence Manaton had watched Reeves passing by that afternoon. The whole of Manaton's furious speech was audible outside the window, for Macdonald himself had seen to it that that window was open a crack. He heard Cavenish go outside again, and the door being banged furiously behind him: Cavenish walked slowly back to the road, with the steps of a man who hesitates as to what he should do, and after a while he began to tramp up and down outside, a hundred yards this way and a hundred yards that.

Macdonald stood where he was, thinking. During the search of the studio that afternoon he had instructed his woman detective to make certain of a fact which he had observed earlier in the day: it was because he wanted to ascertain that one point that he had waited until it was just on black-out time before he had searched. Detective Caroline Lathom had told Macdonald that it was quite easy to get outside the small window in the gallery of the studio and to stand upon the ledge: thus standing a person of average height had their eyes on a level with the window of Mr. Folliner's room.

When the shutters were closed in this room the air-raid warden had had cause to complain that light shone out of a hole in the shutters. Mrs. Tubbs had put this matter right by pasting paper over the hole, but Macdonald had had the paper removed. It then became evident that when the light was burning in Mr. Folliner's bedroom—and the old man had a harsh unshaded bulb—it was possible to see into the room from the window of the gallery in the studio. If anybody had been sufficiently inquisitive to want to get a "close-up" of the occupant of the bedroom, it would have been very easy to put a plank from one window sill to the other and step up close to Mr. Folliner's window. Remembering Mrs. Tubbs' account of Stort's painting of Mr. Folliner, also Miss Stanton's complaints about that gentleman's habit of trespassing, Macdonald thought it more than probable that Stort had thus played "Peeping Tom," and that it was on visual evidence of Mr. Folliner's evening occupation that Listelle had entertained the bar with his account of the "clinking coins." Macdonald doubted if coins had been much in evidence—it was nearly thirty years now since sovereigns had been in common circulation: he also realised that the "peep-show" could not have been observed since the black-out restrictions were imposed, and thus neither Bruce Manaton nor his sister would have had any chance of prying on Mr. Folliner.

Moving quietly along by the studio wall, Macdonald reached the end nearest to the house: here the cord which had belonged to the flag pole flapped dismally above his head. He went and fetched a ladder which he had had brought in, upended it silently, and after listening for a moment or two, he climbed the ladder and caught the loose cord and pulled it. It was not slack: some weight resisted the tension that he put on it—not a very heavy weight; if he had continued to pull he could have hauled the line in. He let the cord go after an experimental tug, leaving it flapping as before, and then climbed down and removed the ladder, putting it inside the back door of the house.

II

After he had replaced the ladder, Macdonald glanced at his watch: the luminous hands pointed to nine-thirty. He went out into the street and listened in the darkness: Robert Cavenish was still there, tramping slowly along about a hundred yards away. As Macdonald waited, a man came silently up to him in the darkness.

"Ward, sir. No one else has come near—only that chap who's walking up and down. Inspector Jenkins is still inside. Says he's nearly through."

The whispered words were spoken close to Macdonald's ear. He replied equally softly:

"Very good. Keep on the alert. It won't be easy: we may be here all night for nothing. Look out for Reeves. He may report later. Drew's on duty at the call-box. I'm going to tell this other fellow to go home."

Ward melted away into the darkness, and Macdonald waited until Cavenish drew level with the gate. Then he went out and caught him up.

"Mr. Cavenish, I think it would be wiser for you to go home. You can't do any good tramping up and down here, and it's a cold night."

Cavenish came to a halt. "The Chief Inspector, isn't it? Sorry if I'm in the way. I'm worried."

"What are you worrying about?"

"Rosanne Manaton. Her brother doesn't know where she is."

"Perhaps she doesn't want him to know where she is. In any case, you can't do anything about it. Better go home. This is my beat to-night, and I can't have people loitering."

"I see. Meaning that if I don't go, you'll take steps to remove me?"

"That's it. Be advised—go home and stay there, and do your thinking by your own fireside. You'll have to give evidence to-morrow."

There was a pause: Macdonald could hear the other man breathing quickly beside him. At last Cavenish said:

"Do you know where she is—Rosanne?"

"Yes. I know. Now, once again, go while the going's good. Good-night."

"You won't tell me—?"

"I have told you everything I'm going to tell you."

"I see. Then good-night."

Cavenish turned away and walked off steadily, southwards. Macdonald returned to number twenty-five and went in at the back door: its hinges moved silently now, and in the darkness no one could see that it was slightly ajar. He waited inside, waited as he had done a hundred times, to see if a "hunch" worked true.

A quarter of an hour later, Macdonald became aware that someone was approaching the door: it wasn't so much hearing, and certainly not sight, which warned his detective faculty of someone at hand. He stepped close to the slightly open door.

A voice spoke, very softly: "Drew, sir: report from C.O. Randall Stort's body has been picked up on the Metropolitan line near Harrow."

Macdonald was silent a second: then he said, "Go back to the box and wait. Reeves may call through. Tell him about Stort and say he's to report here as soon as he can."

"Very good, sir."

Another shadow departed silently, and Macdonald was left with his thoughts—grim thoughts. In his mind's eye he saw a series of pictures, and chief among them were some wall paintings, smeared, obliterated... a mess of paint on a dingy wall.

It was half an hour later that he heard another sound, not in the street this time: the slight scraping came from the wall at the far end of the studio, where Reeves had climbed only that afternoon. Someone was climbing the wall—but not Reeves. The latter would have contrived this activity with much less sound. "A cat had nothing on Reeves," so they said who had been on the trail with him. Macdonald stayed where he was, listening.

The intruder slithered down the wall on the studio side, not very skilfully. Macdonald heard the thump of feet landing on the earth, and a few seconds later footsteps—very quiet footsteps— sounded along by the studio and then some further sounds at the end nearest the house. Then came a slight dragging sound—the cord from the flag pole rattled a little on the corrugated roof as it was disturbed. Silently Macdonald emerged from the back door, but as swiftly drew back. A beam of light shone whitely down the dingy path as the studio door was flung open, and Bruce Manaton's voice shouted: "Who's there? Rosanne, is that you—is that you, I say?"

A man's voice answered, low and urgent.

"No. It's not Rosanne. Shut that door! The light's glaring right out into the road."

"Damn the light! What the hell do you think you're doing? Where is Rosanne?"

"Twenty thousand devils! *Must* you be such a fool? Go inside and shut that door."

"I *won't* go inside…"

"Oh, won't you? Then I'd better come in and talk to you." The other voice, very low and deep, had an ominous note in it. "Come inside and talk there, my friend. It will be better for both of us. Rosanne is not on in this act."

Macdonald, peeping between the cracks of his own door, saw two figures in silhouette against the light of the studio. Then the door was closed as they both went inside.

Macdonald made a spring for the stairs and whistled—a short clear note. Jenkins was upstairs, and Jenkins was a useful fellow in an emergency. He heard Jenkins' answering whistle, and called softly, "There's another party in the studio—come and stand by."

Macdonald himself went outside and moved swiftly to the studio window, the one which he had unlatched when he had helped to black-out that afternoon: he stood there and listened. He could hear the deep voice of the newcomer—a low, soft murmur, but not a word that was spoken was audible: the voice was pitched much too low. Occasionally Bruce Manaton's irritable staccato broke in, but nearly always in question—a querulous demand for information which told Macdonald nothing. He stood there waiting, until he was aware that Jenkins was beside him. Macdonald whispered: "Stand by here. I'm going to see if I can get inside the gallery window."

He slipped quickly along to the further end and balanced a short plank against the wall for a foothold: from here he could reach the projecting sill of the window, and he hauled himself up, absolutely silently. Macdonald had often reflected that he himself would make a very useful cat-burglar. His experience as a rock-climber enabled him to utilise any hand-hold or foothold available, and he had the balance of a cat.

Standing there in the darkness on a very precarious ledge, he set about the business of opening the casement window which Detective Lathom had left unlatched. It was a ticklish business, which meant balancing on one foot with a minimum of space for bending, and one false move or sound would have ruined his project. The window was curtained inside by a heavy woollen curtain: Macdonald knew that he had one advantage—the position in which the two men were sitting in the studio was such that they could not see up into the gallery. All he had to do was to get inside without making any sound. Once the window was open it took all his skill—and muscle—to achieve an entry. Cold though the night was, he sweated as he lowered himself and got one foot inside, every muscle taut until cramp nearly defeated him.

When he was at last inside, both feet on the floor, the black-out curtain still between himself and the rest of the studio, Macdonald took a deep breath. The business of negotiating his silent entry had taken as much effort as any hazardous rock-climb, to say nothing of being vastly more uncomfortable.

He drew the window to behind him, and slipped down on to the floor, conscious that while he had been concentrating on his own gymnastics he had not consciously heard a word of the conversation going on below in the studio. He moved forward softly to the edge of the gallery and parted the curtains a chink so that he could see below. He could just see the top of Bruce Manaton's head, the other man was a little beneath the gallery and thus concealed from Macdonald, but a hand was stretched out holding a whisky bottle, and that same hand poured out half a tumbler of the spirit and pushed it towards Manaton.

"Get outside of that, old man; that'll steady your nerves. Remember this: you've got nothing to worry about, *absolutely nothing*. Things couldn't have gone better. I told you the scheme was foolproof if you would only play your part—and by Gad! you played it well. The evidence stands, and it's indisputable."

The deep bass whisper ceased, and there was another gurgle as the whisky bottle was tilted: Macdonald could smell the spirit in the glasses, so near was he to the drinkers.

"My God, I needed that!" went on the cautious whisper. "I've had all the work to do, remember that." A low, satisfied chuckle followed the lip-smacking of a satisfied drinker. "It was almost incredible the way things worked out," he went on. "I felt as though I was working a puppet-show, pulling the strings and making the puppets dance... It was as near perfection as could be."

Bruce Manaton brought down his glass on to the table with a slam. "Near perfection," he echoed, and his voice was thick, his articulation slurred. "Near—but not perfect. I've been thinking. That rat Stort. If he hears about this, he'll barge in."

"And if he does, what matter? The evidence stands. In any case, he won't. I've been making a few enquiries. Stort won't barge in—nor yet Listelle. They'll tell no tales. Neither of them. I tell you again—*don't worry*. The evidence stands."

Another chuckle sounded below Macdonald, and the clink of a glass.

"You and I have had a poor deal so far in the way of this world's goods," went on the whisperer. "Take you—can you draw, can you paint? I doubt if there's a painter amongst the whole crowd of 'em who can beat you in the handling of your own medium. Go round the modern shows—the London group, the portraitists, any of them. I tell you August John himself couldn't beat the handling of that work of yours on the easel there. What have you got out of it? What sort of life have you had? Take this bloody hole we're sitting in!

Comfort, security, recognition? Pah! one long damned struggle with circumstance. I tell you it sickens me." There was a silence, and then the voice went on: "Some men are content to bow to circumstance, to admit defeat, to put up with poverty… 'like the wretched slave, who with a body filled and vacant mind, gets him to bed, crammed with distressful bread…' Not I, my friend, not I! I've got brains and I've got nerve, and, by hell, I've used them at long last."

A glass was put down on the table, and a chair pushed back.

"'Screw your courage to the sticking point, and we'll not fail'! Now there's this to it. We must get that stuff moved. It was policy to leave it so long, but now it's got to be moved. I've been thinking it out. I'm going to divide it into two lots—one for you and one for me, and we'll dump it in the place I arranged. We can't cash in on it yet—no hurry, above all, no hurry! We'll go on cheese-paring, living on the smell of an oiled rag until the excitement's died down. May be the war will be over. We can go abroad. I've a fancy for South America myself, somewhere where the sun shines. You can have your villa at Capri, or that little place outside Barcelona… the future's ours, if only we keep our heads and stick out the damned present." Again came a chuckle. "I'm glad they searched the place so well. That raw-boned Scot's an efficient devil. I hoped he'd search. Makes me laugh. Now you stay here, old chap. I'm going to haul the line in."

Bruce Manaton stirred and pushed his chair back. "I'm going to keep an eye on you. You're not above swindling your own mother, I know that. Don't imagine I'm going to let you get away with it."

His voice was slurred and sleepy, the voice of a man who was in the quarrelsome stage of drunkenness.

The other replied: "Now don't you get imagining things: haven't I done all the real work in this job? Without me, you'd have finished your life as an unsuccessful painter—gone to a pauper's grave as like as not. With me, the combination of my wits and yours, we've got a future… Remember the future! Drink to the future!—but keep your head now. I'm going to haul that line in… Oh, all right, come if you must, but for God's sake don't make a sound. It's almost certain there's one of those C.I.D. fellows snooping around that house. Put the light out. It's only a step outside, but nobody must hear. Remember, the only danger in the whole business is if we're caught with the stuff on us. Have another drink. It'll steady you."

"I'm not going to have another drink until I know you're playing square. You're trying to make me drunk, hoping I'll go to sleep and leave you to make off with the goods. Oh, no, my friend: you don't trick me that way—and remember this—if you try any tricks I'll see to it that you hang, even though I hang beside you."

"Gently! Gently! No need for that sort of thing between you and me. Having got thus far, 'twere pity to spoil the good work by quarrelling. Come then, come with me—but softly, softly… *chi va piano va sano, chi va sano, va lentano*. Remember, not a sound!"

The light clicked out, and Macdonald was left in blackness. He heard the two men cross the studio and open the front door. He knew that Jenkins was close at hand, that Ward and Drew were on the alert outside. He reached the gallery window and opened it a crack and waited. In his mind was the memory of a grandfather clock with the weights missing: a rope, a pulley and two good weights: an empty chimney shaft and a bundle running up on the end of a line, jerking over the edge of a wide chimney cowl as the line was released and the weights ran down inside the shaft. Now the winding up process was to be put into operation.

Silent at the window, Macdonald heard a box being placed against the side of the studio, very quietly. Then someone mounted it, and there came the tap of the line on the roof, then a tugging dragging sound: there was a little bumping and scuffling, a slithering as a bundle was dragged clear of the cowl and then a swish. A moment later the two men went back into the studio.

Macdonald heard the front door close behind them, and the light was switched on again. He was just about to go down the gallery steps to confront them, when a word from Bruce Manaton brought him to a halt. There was something else he wanted to know. Manaton was at the whisky bottle again: then he said suddenly:

"What about Rosanne?"

The other gave an exclamation of impatience.

"Rosanne? What about her? I told you, she's not on in this act."

Manaton spoke still more slowly, his voice dragging, stuttering a little.

"She was out there... in the black-out. How much does she know?... She guessed, you know... she looked in at the door once too often... If she'd only understand. I did it for Rosanne..."

His voice dragged out into silence, and Macdonald stood still, for the first time a sense of pity in his mind. The other man stood still, and then an ugly burst of profanity flowed from his lips.

"... Rosanne... if she lets us down, I'll strangle her with my own hands, the..."

Macdonald took the stairs in one leap. He knew what was coming now. Manaton, drunk, beside himself, had seized the first weapon which came to his hand—the soda siphon which stood on the table. Before Macdonald could intervene, the other had wrenched the siphon away and brought it crashing down on the painter's head. Blind drunken fury was behind the deadly blow. Bruce Manaton crumpled up, and Macdonald caught him as he fell, crashing against the red-daubed canvas with its portrait of a man in Cardinal's robes.

III

Reeves always had a feeling of satisfaction that his evening ended up with the climax to a case. He had travelled back from Harrow cursing himself bitterly. Reeves was not by nature a boaster; he was a cautious, hard-working, reticent fellow. He could not forget his own voice saying "he shan't outwit me." He felt that he *had* been outwitted, properly, but there was also in his mind a conviction that Macdonald would not have been similarly defeated. "Our Jock will make sense of it," was a firmly rooted belief in Reeves' mind. He made his way from Finchley Road Station to Hollyberry Hill at a great pace and was just going to report at his "point"—the police call-box—when he heard a sound which made him tingle—the shrilling of a police whistle. "Things happening, by gum," was his immediate reaction. On tiptoes, mentally as well as physically, Reeves advanced towards number twenty-five. He heard the sounds of a scuffle in the garden and stamping of feet: a thud told him that someone had gone down in a melee, and he crouched a little, his elbows squared, fists at the ready, almost dancing in the shadows of the wall. He just saw the blackness of a heavy figure pounding along towards him, a man running for his life, grunting as he pounded along. Reeves closed in with a joyous sense of achievement, frustration fled. He tackled at the strategic spot, and the fugitive crashed down, thudding on to the slippery London pavement while Reeves recovered himself like an eel and bestraddled his captive. Drew's voice came out of the darkness:

"Got him? The Chief's inside."

"Yes. I've got him," said Reeves, "and by gum, I enjoyed getting him. This evening owed me something, but it's all square now."

IV

In the studio, a somewhat winded Jenkins found Macdonald.

"I collared him, but he got away—and ran straight into Reeves' arms. That was that. He's a tough lad, our Reeves. So was I, when I was his age. Hullo, he looks bad, Chief."

"Yes. He's finished."

Macdonald stood looking down at Bruce Manaton's body.

"I suppose I ought to have prevented that, Jenkins: I suppose I *could* have prevented it, but I didn't want to. It'll be easier for Rosanne this way."

Jenkins nodded soberly.

"Yes. You're right there—but I've no compunction about the other chap. I reckon it was his father he shot, and the world will be well quit of the pair of them. I've finished going through the old man's papers. He was a hard old devil."

"So, it seems, was his son," replied Macdonald.

CHAPTER FIFTEEN

I

"**S**O WE WERE CAST FOR THE PARTS OF THE TWO MUGS."
Ian Mackellon voiced his disillusionment in a tone which made Macdonald chuckle.

"Few men like to feel that they have been fooled," said the latter, "and Aberdonians like it less than most. You needn't feel so bitter about it. Your presence was requested in the studio on that particular evening because you and Mr. Cavenish were obviously reliable, law-worthy and conscientious men. No police inspector worth his salt could have suspected either of you of corruption. Therein was your value."

Macdonald was sitting in the studio, where he had acceded to Mackellon's request for an exposition of the "Cardinal Crime," as Mackellon called it. Sitting opposite one another across a chessboard, Cavenish and Mackellon listened.

"I think I'll tell you the story from the detective's point of view," said Macdonald, and Cavenish put in gravely:

"We shall be indebted to you, Chief Inspector. It is good of you to spare us the time."

Macdonald caught a glint of humour in Mackellon's hazel eyes, and responded to that.

"Don't be too grateful," he said. "Mackellon will admit that all true Scots like talking—on occasion. We're silent on occasion, especially when we have a job to do, but we talk all right at times. I'm through with a job of work, and I can relax a while—and talk."

He puffed at his pipe for a moment and then began:

"I had the bare facts: an old man had been shot at close quarters in his bed. An empty cash-box and a pistol lay on the floor. A Canadian soldier had been arrested on the spot, and the Special Constable who arrested him said that the soldier had made a bee-line for this studio, as though for a deliberate reason. I sent the camera and fingerprint men into the house to do their job, and then I came in here to consider the assembled company. You remember my own entry on to this stage, I expect."

Mackellon laughed. "I shall never forget it. I liked the manner in which you summed us all up."

"It was an interesting occasion," said Macdonald. "I quite understood why Mr. Verraby had felt that the party looked strange—capable of anything, as he expressed it. Delaunier, in his scarlet trappings, was so dramatic. Manaton so very much the temperamental painter, and the studio so bizarre in effect that the resulting impression was operatic, something far removed from the average of everyday experience. What struck me most was the contrast in type of the two pairs of men I saw there. Two were artists: two were reliable, hard-headed, and, it seemed to me, conscientious citizens."

Mackellon put a word in here: "Are artists never reliable, or hard-headed, or conscientious?"

"Of course they are," replied Macdonald, "but in this case, I summed up Manaton as being unstable: it was true that he behaved well and spoke reasonably, but it seemed to me that he made a deliberate effort, as though he were controlling himself with an end in view. It mattered to him that the impression he should make on me was a good one, though he hadn't cared, apparently, to thus impress the special constable. Thinking it over afterwards, I found myself wondering if Manaton were drunk—quietly, unostentatiously drunk."

Mackellon nodded. "Drunk—or doped. When he had drunk enough whisky to make most men insensible, I have heard Manaton talk and argue much more lucidly than when he was sober."

Macdonald went on: "Delaunier was an actor: he acted deliberately, and it was difficult to judge the man behind the acting. Well, I saw Bruce Manaton's portrait. It was good—very good it seemed to me. I had just heard of Delaunier. I knew this—neither of the two was successful, an unknown painter, an obscure actor—but both men with energy and ability. In addition there was Manaton's sister—reserved, cold, steady, and determined to say nothing at all. She watched, and waited—a difficult person to assess. Quite obviously, being Bruce Manaton's sister, and at the same time being a woman of sensibility and orderliness, she must have had a hard life. Sisters of men like Bruce Manaton do have hard lives, if they try to retain their self-respect, as Rosanne Manaton did." Macdonald paused: "I'm being long-winded over this, but I'm interested in my own recapitulation here. I saw this studio, and the kitchen there. I saw the efforts of one person to uphold the niceties and decencies of life—cleanliness, orderliness, grace—and on the other hand, squalor. The brother did not mind squalor. He was used to it. The sister was not."

Cavenish spoke here, in his sober, conscientious way.

"I'm glad you saw all that. I did. Rosanne Manaton has struggled against heavy odds, but she never complained and never gave in."

"Well, there it was," said Macdonald. "I took your evidence: it amounted to the fact that you four men had been in the studio, within sight of one another, the whole evening. Delaunier was most emphatic over this: he even recapitulated the chess moves. However, during the evening's sitting, Delaunier had moved about the studio occasionally—the chess players were used to that and took no notice. Also there was a lay figure on the floor. I merely noted the possibilities. Miss Manaton had looked inside the studio several times: she had also been outside to inspect the black-out. She had nothing to say—and the key of Mr. Folliner's house was on the kitchen table." Again Macdonald paused, and then went on: "I needn't stress all the details of our search in the house: the outstanding facts were the pistol—old Folliner's own—an empty cash-box, and a postcard from Neil Folliner saying he was calling to see his uncle that evening. The postcard I regarded as exhibit A. It dated the crime. The old man was shot that evening *because* his nephew was coming, and that nephew could act as scapegoat. It was an assumption on my part, but it was right. The man who left the postcard for us to find over-acted. It was a mistake. The first thing I asked myself was, 'Who could have got hold of that postcard?' The answers were obvious—Mrs. Tubbs, or the studio tenants. Very often in these days, when inexperienced people are delivering mails, letters for separate addresses may get delivered into one and the same letter-box. It was quite probable that the studio people could take letters from the new postman—or postwoman—and obtain both the studio mail and that for the house. It did look to me as though the studio people could have got hold of that postcard, while it was very improbable that Verraby could have. Another point about that postcard." He turned to Cavenish. "You remember that I asked you to write down exactly what Neil Folliner had said while he was in the studio. I asked Mackellon to do the same thing. You both wrote down that Neil Folliner had said 'I wrote to uncle and told him I was coming this evening.' Bruce Manaton stated that Folliner had said 'I sent uncle a postcard'—so somebody in the studio knew about that postcard."

Mackellon nodded. "Yes," he said. "It's points like that give a liar away. I've always maintained that it's very difficult to lie consistently and to get away with it."

Macdonald nodded. "That's quite true: it's also true that it is on *little* points that a liar trips up. Well, here are two small points. Mrs. Tubbs had left the key of Mr. Folliner's house in the studio not once but several times. An impression of it could have been made very easily. The studio people could have got hold of Neil Folliner's postcard. Next, to get on with Mrs. Tubbs' evidence. I liked Mrs. Tubbs—liked her at once and whole-heartedly. She will always embody for me the spirit which makes the wizened little Cockney one of the grandest characters in the world."

Mackellon nodded. "You're right," he said. "I've often thought it's Mrs. Tubbs who's really beating Hitler. He doesn't understand Mrs. Tubbs. You can call that sentiment if you like, but it's true."

"It's true enough," said Macdonald soberly. "Now Mrs. Tubbs had been keeping that old man alive because she couldn't bear to think of him starving. I've Neil Folliner's evidence that that is true—it wasn't made up by Mrs. Tubbs. She would not have done that if she had suspected that the old man was wealthy. She knew he was a skinflint, and she said that she made him pay her something when he had got tenants in the studio. That was just: Mrs. Tubbs struck me as having her own clear ideas of justice, and not bad ideas either. I did not think it probable that she had kept an old man from starving in order to rob him and kill him: neither did I believe that she knew he was wealthy and had spread the news abroad among her own friends. She called him 'the poor old misery,' and that was her attitude to him, an attitude of compassion, and it rang true. Now Mrs. Tubbs told me one or two interesting things *en passant*, and one of the most interesting was that the previous tenant of the studio, a man named Stort, had painted a picture of old Mr. Folliner with his hands clutching money which he was counting over. 'I did it from memory, Ma,' said Stort—and Mrs. Tubbs resented the familiarity of that word 'Ma'! She did not know how much interested I was in her recital. How had Stort seen old Folliner so that he could paint that picture from memory, and how had he got the idea of him counting money like a miser? Incidentally, I've got that painting to show in court—Reeves ran it to earth for me. Here is a photograph of it."

Macdonald showed them the reproduction of "Peep-Show," Mackellon exclaimed aloud:

"Good Lord! How did he get the detail?"

Macdonald replied, "The detail is absolutely accurate. That is a picture of old Folliner sitting up in his own bed, and it was painted by a man with an accurate memory. Stort *saw* old Folliner sitting up in bed counting his money, not once but many times."

Macdonald then recounted how it was possible to see into Mr. Folliner's bedroom from the gallery window of the studio.

"Of course, I'm putting the fact of finding the picture and of discovering the means of 'peeping' out of order in the time sequence of my own investigation, but Mrs. Tubbs told me about the picture on the evening of the murder."

Mackellon smiled. "In fact your thoughts were directed more and more towards the studio."

Macdonald nodded. "Yes. I saw ever more clearly the value of the two incorruptible witnesses. As I heard Delaunier say later 'the evidence stands.' I won't weary you with an account of my interview with Mr. Verraby. Concerning him, at least, I felt in agreement with Manaton when he said 'We did not like him.' I'll leave him out for the moment. Jenkins worked well into the night examining deceased's papers—and I did a lot of thinking. The next morning I saw Neil Folliner, and I then examined the house in detail in daylight. Three points of interest emerged: one was the existence of some portraits on the walls of the sitting-room. These portraits had been painted out very carefully and were obliterated: one was the existence of a decrepit grandfather clock, minus its weights and chains: one was the view of the studio roof from the first floor of the house, showing a collapsed flag pole and some yards of cord flapping around the studio walls and roof close by the disused chimney-pot."

Cavenish put out a protesting hand. "This is where I get lost," he said. "I've followed all your previous argument, and followed it with intense interest, but the three points you have just mentioned baffle me completely. I'm no good at puzzles."

"If you had been doing my job, you would have asked yourself just the same questions as I did," said Macdonald. "Obviously the first question was: Who was the murderer? Next, what had happened to the contents of his cash-box? As Inspector Jenkins worked through Mr. Folliner's papers, it became increasingly evident that a large amount of money had disappeared."

Ian Mackellon put in a word here. "Obviously one wondered about that," he said. "Assuming that the suspects were Neil Folliner and Mr. Verraby, as we did assume at first, it seemed plain that they would not have risked keeping the loot on them. They would have had to hide it somewhere."

Macdonald nodded. "That was it. Now I did not limit my suspicions to Young Folliner and Verraby—for reasons I have told you in part. I suspected that the secret lay somewhere in the studio party, improbable though that may have seemed. The point was: where was the loot? I guessed that it would not be in any obvious place: it also seemed certain that only a very short time could have been spent on concealing it. How could a man secrete a large bundle of bank notes so that they could escape an expert search? I have known valuables concealed in a container like a thermos flask and sunk in a cistern—but that method was not used. Certainly not burying, nor the dug-out. Well, there was a disused chimney, as you can see for yourselves. It is blocked this end, but the wide cowl of the chimney was open. There was cord—from the flag post—and the weights of the grandfather clock were missing. It seemed to me that with time to fix a pulley in the chimney-pot, if the weights from the clock were attached to one end of the line and put inside the chimney-pot, those weights would be capable of hoisting up a packet attached to the other end of the line and pulling that packet into hiding inside the chimney-pot. It's the grandfather clock idea, the weights do the work. Mechanically, it's a simple contrivance. The pulley is fixed in the chimney and the weights will run down and hoist up a lesser weight than themselves: a sufficient over-plus of cord is necessary to have a length of line to secure outside the chimney-pot, so that it is possible to recover the package inside by hauling on the line."

Mackellon nodded. "Yes, I follow that idea all right; though I should never have tumbled to it because the weights of the grandfather clock were missing."

"Neither did I, not in that way," replied Macdonald. "Detection isn't based on brilliant flashes of intuition—at least, mine isn't. It's based on a reconstruction of possibilities. If you assume that somebody has hidden something, the only thing to do is to consider every conceivable hiding place at their disposal, as though one had to hide the object oneself. Well, that clears the ground a little. Now I'm going back to the beginning, to the studio party. Bearing in mind that the latch-key could have been obtained by any member of that party on previous occasions, and that a postcard had been mentioned, the next problem was which member or members of that party could have done the dirty work. Of course there was Miss Manaton, but if she had been guilty I don't think she would have stated that she had been outside. It wasn't necessary for her to say so. There was no other evidence to show that she had been outside. She could have said 'I was in the kitchen all the time, except when I was in the studio,' and there would have been no means of disproving that statement. No. If the studio party were involved, I thought it much more probable that something much more subtle had been evolved. The situation appealed to me. Here were four men, all of them stating that they had been in the studio from 7.30 onwards in each other's company. Now the very fact that two of those men were reliable conscientious citizens made me more than ever inquisitive. It seemed so plain that the chess players had been imported to give a feeling of confidence to the investigator: they were unimpeachable. It was a clever idea."

Mackellon wriggled.

"Confound you, don't rub it in," he protested. "I've admitted that we were mugs—just plain mugs, done by a confidence trick."

Macdonald chuckled. "I enquired into your *bona fides* later, that I admit, but the situation as I saw it was this. The two of you had been playing chess. Neither of you could have left the chess-board without it being obvious to your partner, to the painter, and to the sitter. Four men conspiring together?—and four ill-assorted men at that? I thought not. Next, could the painter have absented himself for ten minutes without the chess players noticing? Again, I thought not. Bruce Manaton stood in front of that canvas, occasionally moving back to get a fresh focus, occasionally speaking to his model. He was directly in Mackellon's line of vision. He *must* have been there all the time. Finally, there was Delaunier."

"And we assured you that Delaunier was in here the whole time," said Cavenish.

"No. As a matter of fact, you were both very conscientious in your evidence," said Macdonald. "You did not pretend that you had

had your eyes on Delaunier all the time: you said—and I realised that it was true—that you had been concentrating on your game. Delaunier is a chess player himself: he had played with both of you. He *knew* that you were players who concentrated on your game—and I know that a good game of chess can absorb the attention of the players utterly. Delaunier counted on this fact. He knew that you took no notice of him when he moved in the intervals of his posing: he also knew that you would be vaguely aware of the Cardinal's scarlet figure sitting in that chair. Delaunier took a risk—and it came off. Once, during that sitting, he got up to stretch, moved behind the easel as though to examine the drawing, took off his scarlet robe and with Manaton's help slipped it on the lay figure. In another moment that scarlet-clad lay figure was safely in the Spanish chair, the Cardinal's hat upon its head. The risk had been justified: the two chess players had their eyes glued to their board, their minds intent on their game to the exclusion of all else. Probably the two players made a conscious effort to ignore the movements of the painter and his model: they were aware of the scarlet-clad figure, of the painter's occasional comment; the sitting went on, the chess game went on. Within ten minutes—at the outside—Delaunier was back in his place. He must have felt very satisfied. He had planned carefully, and his plan had worked."

Cavenish sighed, but Mackellon said: "Of course I ought to kick myself round and round the room. This trick was played under our very noses, and we never tumbled to it. We just played chess."

Macdonald replied: "You've got to remember that Delaunier counted upon the qualities he knew in you two men. He *knew* you concentrated on your game. It was as though he knew that whatever you did, you would do it thoroughly. He chose for his witnesses two men of acknowledged integrity, thoughtful, hard-working fellows, whose habit was to concentrate on one thing at a time. You must admit that it was clever of him."

"Oh, clever—yes," said Mackellon. "It's the sort of cleverness I shall never forget."

"Don't let it embitter you," said Macdonald, "and while we are here, let us re-enact the game. Reeves is here to pose in the Cardinal's scarlet. I will be the painter. Will you and Cavenish try to continue your game? Black to move and mate in four moves. I know that it's impossible for you to lose yourselves in the game as you did that night, but you can keep your eyes on the board, and Cavenish can do his best to avoid being beaten in four moves. Will you try it?"

"We will," said Mackellon. "Check to your king, Cavenish."

II

A scarlet-clad figure sat again in the high-backed chair. Macdonald stood at the easel. "Chin up: to the right a little," he said.

The Cardinal got up. "A rest, my friend," he proclaimed. He moved behind the easel. Mackellon, his eyes on the board, murmured "check." Cavenish moved his hand to interpose his knight between his king and the attacking bishop, and then hesitated. A scarlet blur moved across the platform and became part of the pattern—easel, tall chair, posing figure. The "painter" said "Further round—head up... right."

"Check," murmured Mackellon again, sweeping away the knight. There was a dead silence. The "painter" stood at his easel. Mackellon bent forward over the board with a gleam in his hazel eyes, and Cavenish pondered with upraised hand as though he were in the presence of a miraculous apparition. Then, abruptly, he seized his one remaining piece, a bishop, moved it diagonally right up the board and took Mackellon's attacking queen.

"Damn!" said the latter abruptly. "I'm not thinking of what I'm doing It's..."

"Gentlemen," said Macdonald, "will you kindly give me your attention now."

Cavenish chuckled. "You've saved my game, Chief Inspector. For the one and only time in our acquaintance I've caught Mackellon napping."

"And what about my demonstration?" asked Macdonald.

Ian Mackellon laughed as he looked round. Reeves was sitting in the Cardinal's chair again, and the lay figure was on the floor behind the easel.

"Yes," said Mackellon. "You win, Chief Inspector. Even under those conditions I did not realise the imposture. I was aware of the movement, but it didn't convey anything to me. So easily can one be fooled."

III

Macdonald sat again beside the chess-board.

"So you see it was quite possible, given those particular conditions. I pondered over it for a long time, and I tried to fit other pieces into the jig-saw assuming that Delaunier was the real culprit, with Bruce Manaton as accessory. There were the smeared-out portraits on the walls of number 25: These had undoubtedly been painted by Stort, the previous tenant of this studio. It seemed to me that one of those pictures might well have been a portrait of Delaunier or of Manaton, and that they had been obliterated to avoid the police seeing them and drawing conclusions from them."

Mackellon gave an exclamation: "But Delaunier *knew* Stort. I heard him say so long ago when I first knew him. I reminded him—Delaunier—of that fact when he came to see Cavenish the other evening."

"Did you?" said Macdonald. "You couldn't have guessed what would be the results of that reminder. Delaunier knew, in his own heart, that Stort was a danger to him. It was through Stort that Delaunier knew of old Folliner's habit of counting his treasure when he was safe in bed. Your mention of Stort brought that danger closer. As soon as he had left you that evening Delaunier went and found Stort at his favourite pub, stood him enough drinks to make him half-drunk, and then went back with him to Harrow on the Metropolitan Railway. They were in an empty compartment, and when the train stopped outside the station, Delaunier opened the carriage door on the wrong side of the train, and Stort stepped out, or was pushed out, on to the live rail."

"Oh Lord!" said Mackellon softly. "One should never say anything…"

"It's not human nature not to say anything," said Macdonald. "Don't worry over that, it would have happened, in all probability, without your prompting. Incidentally, I wasted valuable time over tracing Listelle, only to learn later he had been killed in an air raid. I was having Delaunier watched, though he didn't know it. He came straight back here: he probably realised that things were going awry—and the rest followed."

Cavenish sat looking down at the chess men. "I suppose Delaunier—and Manaton—planned it just for the money, the miser's hoard," he said.

"Yes, in the main, though there's more to it than that," said Macdonald. "When Jenkins had finished going through old Folliner's papers, he found records of Albert Folliner's marriage in 1893. His wife left him not much more than a year later, taking her infant son with her. We have evidence from an old retired chemist nearby that Folliner's son came to see his father when the son was about twenty years of age, and there are letters to the father from the son, asking for financial assistance, at the same period. The son was on the stage—and the name he had taken was André Delaunier."

"Full circle," said Cavenish. "It's a ghastly story, but one finds it difficult to be sorry for either of them, the father or the son."

"The actual relationship has nothing to do with the actual detection," said Macdonald. "It was discovered after things had come to a head. The most interesting thing in the detecting part was working out the possibility of the studio party—the actual relevance of the evidence given by trustworthy witnesses. Bruce Manaton had been a drug-addict at one time, the associate of other degenerates. His sister saved him from going under completely, and tried to pull him up and keep him going, but he was an embittered and disappointed man. Delaunier was also unsuccessful in his profession, and he made one last desperate throw to try to obtain his father's wealth. He worked out the scheme, and Manaton was accessory. Delaunier had a key of the house: he went in, shot the old man, seized the contents of the cash-box, put them in a waterproof case, fastened it to the cord and let the previously arranged weights do the job of hauling the bundle into safe-keeping in the chimney. Then he came in here, resumed his scarlet trappings and his pose—and you continued to play chess."

"What about the sound of the shot?" asked Mackellon.

Macdonald laughed. "I don't know. I never believed that anyone in here noticed it. I know that there were fog signals being let off that night at the entrance to the tunnels. Considering that old Folliner's room was both shuttered and curtained, I think it probable that the shot was no more noticeable than the fog signals. Delaunier's insistence on having heard it was pre-arranged and over-acted. It drew attention to himself by insisting that *he* was on the stage, so to speak—in here—when the shot was heard." Macdonald paused, and then added: "I'm not giving evidence here, and my opinion is worth no more than any other witnesses. I think it probable that Rosanne Manaton heard the shot when she was outside: she may even have heard Delaunier pass her in the dark. That was why she ran away—to avoid giving evidence. She *knew* that if Delaunier was involved, her brother was involved, too. When she left here that evening, she went into hiding with a friend out at Great Missenden. Fortunately her evidence isn't necessary: Delaunier has provided enough evidence and to spare. He killed Bruce Manaton before my eyes."

"Thank God he did," said Cavenish slowly. "One day Rosanne will be able to put all this horror behind her."

There was silence, and then Mackellon asked suddenly:

"Did you suspect us—Cavenish and myself—of being in the plot?"

"No, never," replied Macdonald. "I was quite sure all the time that Delaunier had chosen you for a part, and he made no mistake in choosing his players. You were two incorruptible witnesses. With you giving evidence, he felt absolutely safe."

"Two honest mugs," said Mackellon sadly, and Macdonald rose to his feet and laughed a little.

"Have it your own way. If I'm not dreaming, your king is in check to your opponent's bishop." He turned to Cavenish.

"Good luck!—and happy days in future."

"Thank you, very much indeed," replied Cavenish.

And on that note of gratitude from the older of his "incorrupt-ible witnesses," Macdonald left the studio.

THE END

BRITISH LIBRARY CRIME CLASSICS

The Cornish Coast Murder	JOHN BUDE
The Lake District Murder	JOHN BUDE
Death on the Cherwell	MAVIS DORIEL HAY
Murder Underground	MAVIS DORIEL HAY
The Female Detective	ANDREW FORRESTER
A Scream in Soho	JOHN G. BRANDON
Mystery in White	J. JEFFERSON FARJEON
Murder in Piccadilly	CHARLES KINGSTON
The Sussex Downs Murder	JOHN BUDE
Capital Crimes	ED. MARTIN EDWARDS
Antidote to Venom	FREEMAN WILLS CROFTS
The Hog's Back Mystery	FREEMAN WILLS CROFTS
The Notting Hill Mystery	CHARLES WARREN ADAMS
Resorting to Murder	ED. MARTIN EDWARDS
Death of an Airman	CHRISTOPHER ST JOHN SPRIGG
Quick Curtain	ALAN MELVILLE
Death of Anton	ALAN MELVILLE
Thirteen Guests	J. JEFFERSON FARJEON
The Z Murders	J. JEFFERSON FARJEON
The Santa Klaus Murder	MAVIS DORIEL HAY
Silent Nights	ED. MARTIN EDWARDS
Death on the Riviera	JOHN BUDE
Murder of a Lady	ANTHONY WYNNE
Murder at the Manor	ED. MARTIN EDWARDS
Serpents in Eden	ED. MARTIN EDWARDS
Calamity in Kent	JOHN ROWLAND
Death in the Tunnel	MILES BURTON
The Secret of High Eldersham	MILES BURTON
The 12.30 from Croydon	FREEMAN WILLS CROFTS
Sergeant Cluff Stands Firm	GIL NORTH
The Cheltenham Square Murder	JOHN BUDE
The Methods of Sergeant Cluff	GIL NORTH
Mystery in the Channel	FREEMAN WILLS CROFTS
Death of a Busybody	GEORGE BELLAIRS
The Poisoned Chocolates Case	ANTHONY BERKELEY
Crimson Snow	ED. MARTIN EDWARDS
The Dead Shall be Raised & Murder of a Quack	GEORGE BELLAIRS
Verdict of Twelve	RAYMOND POSTGATE
Scarweather	ANTHONY ROLLS
Family Matters	ANTHONY ROLLS
Miraculous Mysteries	ED. MARTIN EDWARDS
The Incredible Crime	LOIS AUSTEN-LEIGH
Continental Crimes	ED. MARTIN EDWARDS
Death Makes a Prophet	JOHN BUDE
The Long Arm of the Law	ED. MARTIN EDWARDS
Portrait of a Murderer	ANNE MEREDITH
Seven Dead	J. JEFFERSON FARJEON
Foreign Bodies	ED. MARTIN EDWARDS
Somebody at the Door	RAYMOND POSTGATE
Bats in the Belfry	E.C.R. LORAC
Fire in the Thatch	E.C.R. LORAC
Blood on the Tracks	ED. MARTIN EDWARDS
The Murder of My Aunt	RICHARD HULL
Excellent Intentions	RICHARD HULL
Weekend at Thrackley	ALAN MELVILLE
The Arsenal Stadium Mystery	LEONARD GRIBBLE
The Division Bell Mystery	ELLEN WILKINSON
The Belting Inheritance	JULIAN SYMONS
The Colour of Murder	JULIAN SYMONS
The Christmas Card Crime	ED. MARTIN EDWARDS
Murder by Matchlight	E.C.R. LORAC
Smallbone Deceased	MICHAEL GILBERT
Death in Captivity	MICHAEL GILBERT
Death Has Deep Roots	MICHAEL GILBERT
Surfeit of Suspects	GEORGE BELLAIRS
Murder in the Mill-Race	E.C.R. LORAC
Deep Waters	ED. MARTIN EDWARDS
Fell Murder	E.C.R. LORAC
The Body in the Dumb River	GEORGE BELLAIRS
It Walks by Night	JOHN DICKSON CARR
The Measure of Malice	ED. MARTIN EDWARDS
The Christmas Egg	MARY KELLY
Death in Fancy Dress	ANTHONY GILBERT
Castle Skull	JOHN DICKSON CARR
Death in White Pyjamas & Death Knows No Calendar	JOHN BUDE
Settling Scores	ED. MARTIN EDWARDS
Crossed Skis	CAROL CARNAC
The Spoilt Kill	MARY KELLY
The Woman in the Wardrobe	PETER SHAFFER
The Man Who Didn't Fly	MARGOT BENNETT
Checkmate to Murder	E.C.R. LORAC
The Progress of a Crime	JULIAN SYMONS
A Surprise for Christmas	ED. MARTIN EDWARDS
The Lost Gallows	JOHN DICKSON CARR

ALSO AVAILABLE

The Story of Classic Crime in 100 Books	MARTIN EDWARDS
The Pocket Detective: 100+ Puzzles	KATE JACKSON
The Pocket Detective 2: 100+ More Puzzles	KATE JACKSON

Many of our titles are also available in eBook, large print and audio editions